A Candlelight Ecstasy Romance®

MARTHA BEGAN, "I DIDN'T KNOW THINGS WOULD BE THIS WAY."

"What way is that?" Greg asked, crossing his arms over his bare chest.

"I see you so seldom. And now, having to do those undignified commercials! My contract doesn't say I have to promote Martha's Inns wearing a tavern wench's costume. I'm supposed to be a food expert endorsing your restaurants, not a . . . a . . ."

"Be reasonable, Martha. The gown is a little low-cut, but people won't buy food from a stuffy lecturer. All I'm doing is merchandising my business in the usual way."

"I thought Martha's Inns would be different."

"Are you saying you find working for me distasteful?"

"Yes! I hate being your pin-up girl!"

CANDLELIGHT ECSTASY ROMANCES®

ADD A DASH OF LOVE

Barbara Andrews

A CANDLELIGHT ECSTASY ROMANCE®

Published by
Dell Publishing Co., Inc.
1 Dag Hammarskjold Plaza
New York, New York 10017

Dell ® TM 681510, Dell Publishing Co., Inc.

Candlelight Ecstasy Romance®, 1,203,540, is a registered
trademark of Dell Publishing Co., Inc., New York, New York.

ISBN: 0-440-10017-8

Printed in the United States of America

First printing—November 1985

To Our Readers:

We have been delighted with your enthusiastic response to Candlelight Ecstasy Romances®, and we thank you for the interest you have shown in this exciting series.

In the upcoming months we will continue to present the distinctive, sensuous love stories you have come to expect only from Ecstasy. We look forward to bringing you many more books from your favorite authors and also the very finest work from new authors of contemporary romantic fiction.

As always, we are striving to present the unique, absorbing love stories that you enjoy most—books that are more than ordinary romance. Your suggestions and comments are always welcome. Please write to us at the address below.

Sincerely,

The Editors
Candlelight Romances
1 Dag Hammarskjold Plaza
New York, New York 10017

CHAPTER ONE

The click of her high heels on the old brick sidewalk sounded brisk, but Martha's mood was anything but jaunty. Carrying a bulky cardboard box made the three blocks to the historical Alexandria row house she shared with her mother seem like three miles. She could've cheerfully thrown a stick of dynamite at the deserted truck that blocked the narrow one-way alley leading to her precious parking space! Everyone in Alexandria seemed to have Friday evening guests whose cars were taking up all the parking places on the street, so she'd had to park three blocks away.

Why had the Sugar Glen Historical Society stowed 300 years worth of family recipes in one heavy box? she wondered plaintively. In spite of the anxiety that lurked in the back of her mind these days, she looked forward to sorting through and authenticating the culinary history of the Sugar Glen women, several of whom had early colonial roots. If their old family recipes were as promising as they sounded, Martha could put together one of the finest cookbooks offered by any historical society in Virginia. What she didn't relish was telling her mother that she'd only receive a small advance on the book. The society members had stretched their resources to the limit restoring the home of the district's first congressional representative, Silas Strucker, and were, in fact, hoping that sales of the cookbook would loosen the financial bind they were in. They did, however, compensate for the token advance with a generous royalty offer. Martha had accepted after a long meeting with the board, pleased with the opportunity to do original research but disappointed because the front money wouldn't be nearly enough to put her mother's mind at rest. It would be more than a year before the royalties produced any income.

Passing the weathered brick front of her home, she took in the crumbled corner of the front step and the peeling green paint on the shutters that flanked the single tall window beside the door. She wondered, as she often did, when they'd be able to afford to repair the house. Since the Bicentennial, most of the houses in Old Town had undergone a major restoration. The Graves's home was the only one on their short block that hadn't been given a facelift. Her father, who hadn't lived to celebrate the nation's two hundredth birthday, had been spared seeing his cherished family home grow more and more shabby while new, affluent neighbors moved in and restored the surrounding gracious three-story houses built flush with the brick walls in this oldest part of the city.

Unlocking an iron gate, Martha set the box down and pushed it ahead of her into a paved alleyway. After closing the gate behind her, she resumed carrying the box full of recipes. The passageway to the walled garden was so narrow, she had to watch her elbows to keep from scraping them on the brick walls on either side, and she wondered how the original lady of the house had managed to pass through it with great flounced skirts. She didn't even glance at the old boxwood tree with its circular weathered-wood seat or the high rust-colored brick wall that made the courtyard in back of the house a private sanctuary. In years past she'd eagerly anticipated spring, hardly able to wait until the little garden bloomed with colorful azaleas, camellias, and climbing roses. This year she hoped spring would be late in coming. In a few more months her mother might be well enough to tend her much-loved flowers.

"Mother?" she called as she entered the house.

Martha left the box and her shoulder bag on the kitchen table and walked through the narrow dining area into the front room, repeating her call.

"Up here, dear!"

"What are you doing upstairs at this time of day?" Martha stood at the bottom of the stairs, absentmindedly fingering the graceful wooden banister, which along with the authentic colonial fireplace in the kitchen, was the most beautiful feature of the house.

"Changing my clothes," her mother answered.

"Mother," Martha sighed as she ran up the steps. "Why didn't you wait until I got home?"

"Don't worry." Fleury Graves moved through her bedroom door with as much grace as her crutches allowed and smiled at her only child. "I slid up and down the steps on my bottom. No chance of falling that way."

"Your green velvet dress? What's the occasion?"

"Lydia's sister is visiting. We're going to have a table of bridge here. I'm so tired of dowdy old housecoats, I felt like dressing up."

"You look lovely."

It was true. At fifty-three Fleury was almost double her daughter's age of twenty-eight, but her face had the kind of classic delicacy that doesn't seem to age. Her long hair, more silvery now than blond, was coiled around her head. The weight she'd lost since her automobile accident made her seem more fragile, and Martha frequently had to stifle an impulse to be overly protective. At five feet six, with full breasts and rounded hips, Martha felt oversized compared to her mother.

Thinking her own name too frivolous, Fleury had given her daughter a dignified one. Martha thought her name looked fine on the cover of the colonial-era cookbooks she wrote, but for everyday use it was a bit stodgy. Her thoughtfulness, intelligence, and early maturity had seemingly discouraged friends and family alike from pinning a nickname on her.

"Just let me get down the steps, and you can tell me all about Sugar Glen," her mother said. "I don't want to slide down on my seat in this dress."

Automatically going first and watching her mother descend on the crutches, Martha didn't breathe comfortably until they were both standing in the ground-floor hallway. She didn't even want to think about what would happen if her mother's crutches slipped on the stairs.

"Oh, I almost forgot!" Fleury said. "Rhonda called. She said it's absolutely urgent that you call her the minute you get home."

Martha smiled, knowing that everything was absolutely urgent to her best friend from high school. She probably wanted to arrange a blind date. Married now, as most of Martha's friends were, Rhonda had made it a personal crusade to recruit Martha into the matrimonial ranks. Her husband, John Van Loos, seemed to have an inexhaustible supply of unmarried friends, but Martha wasn't going to be lured into another of Rhonda's matchmaking schemes. She was much too tired for it this weekend and her mother's bridge game meant she could retreat to her third-floor bedroom, which also served as her office, and plunge into the box of Sugar Glen recipes.

"I'm sure tomorrow is soon enough to return her call."

"Dear, I promised you'd phone the minute you got home."

"Mother, she probably wants to fix me up with someone."

"No, I'm sure it's not that. She said it was important."

Fleury was never quite able to disguise the fact that she was encouraging Rhonda's efforts. Before her accident, she'd been screening all the young attorneys in the legal firm where she'd worked as the senior partner's private secretary.

"I'll call later, after I've fixed some dinner for us."

"Oh, not for me, dear. Lydia insisted on bringing some of her crabmeat salad. It's not my favorite, but I couldn't hurt her feelings by refusing. There's still a little roast left for you," she added somewhat apologetically.

"Cold roast is fine. I was too wrapped up in the meeting to eat much lunch, so anything will taste good."

"Was the traffic heavy?" Even before her accident, Fleury had viewed highway driving as a dangerous foray into battle.

"About what you'd expect on a Friday evening. Everyone who isn't nailed to a desk trying to get away from Washington."

"Oh, Rhonda did say something about a job opportunity for you. Maybe you should call her now."

Fleury was even more worried than Martha about her winter-long absence from work and their latest financial predicament.

"All right, but if she wants me to go out with some engineer that John dragged home, I'm going to stay right here instead and kibitz your bridge game. I may even give Lydia secret signals."

"You terrible brat!" her mother said, laughing. "That's

13

as bad as the time I took you to the polls with me and you announced who I was going to pick for president."

"I was six years old, and you weren't the only one in the precinct voting for that candidate!"

"Harriet Gordon was sitting right there working the election. I was never asked to substitute in her bridge group again."

"You can't stand Harriet Gordon!"

"Well, she makes nice popovers." Her mother grinned and made her way carefully to the couch, suppressing a small groan as she lowered herself to the plump, flowered cushion. "I hate to ask, but after you call, would you mind setting up the bridge table for me?"

"Not at all." Martha went to phone her friend, deciding she'd rather return the call than have her mother remember to ask about the cookbook advance.

Rhonda was the only person Martha knew with natural auburn hair. Tall and heavy-boned, with a husky voice and freckled features, she was as forceful as she was good-natured. As friends in high school and roommates in college, Martha supplied the ideas and Rhonda the enthusiasm to carry them out. Without her boisterous friend, Martha's life would've been much tamer. Unlike many friendships, theirs hadn't been overshadowed by marriage. Rhonda's husband traveled a great deal as a representative for a container corporation and Martha frequently went with her friend on antique-buying trips to restock Rhonda's aunt's Old Town shop.

"Rhonda, hi."

"Marth—are you doing anything tonight—right now?"

"A few things, yes," Martha said cautiously.

"Drop everything! I'm having a wine and cheese party and you have to get over here immediately!"

14

"I just got home. I need a bath. By the time I wash my hair and get dressed, your party will be over."

"Listen," Rhonda said, lowering her voice to a conspiratorial whisper, "I can't talk now. I'm in the kitchen. But this isn't what you think. I think there's an opportunity for you to earn some real money."

"Why are you being so mysterious?"

"People are here already. You haven't heard anything new from the insurance company, have you?"

"Only that they won't pay half of mother's surgery bill." She didn't try to disguise her worry; Rhonda knew her too well.

"More people are coming. I have to go. Just come! Promise me!"

"Rhonda, I have to help Mother get ready for bridge and—"

"This is urgent! If you don't come, I'm coming over there after you!"

Her friend's pleading whisper succeeded in making Martha very curious. "It'll probably be an hour before I can get there."

"Forget your hair. Make it half an hour!"

"Well, I'll try."

Martha was even more intrigued. When her friend cooked up something that was supposed to be romantic, she overflowed with advice on how Martha should fix her hair and dress.

"You just have to come!" Rhonda added urgently.

The phone went dead, but Martha stood frowning at it for a moment. Coyness wasn't her friend's style; she really did seem anxious about something.

"She wants me to rush over for a wine and cheese party," Martha explained to her mother.

"You just forget I mentioned the bridge table. Lydia can get it. She's always willing to do things for me."

"I'll get it. There's no rush."

"Absolutely not! I promise I won't try to get it myself. You hurry upstairs and wash your hair."

"Mother!"

"Oh, dear, I did sound like a mother, didn't I? Of course, your hair still looks fine."

"It's windblown and needs a shampoo." Martha smiled wearily and ran her fingers through blond-streaked light brown hair. "I guess if I'm going out . . ."

Carrying the box up to her cozy third-floor hideaway, she was tempted to ignore Rhonda's urgency and her mother's prodding. It would be so pleasant to soak in the big claw-foot tub on the second floor, then start reading through the treasured old recipes. Her feet were tired from a full day of moving around in the high gray suede heels that complimented her tweed suit. The prospect of standing for several more hours conversing with the crowd of strangers Rhonda had most likely gathered at short notice was far from appealing.

Curiosity won out. Thirty minutes later she was dressed in her blue wool dress, the aquamarine shade making her lightly shadowed eyes look rounder and bluer. She had a choice of walking three blocks to get her little Honda, then trying to find a parking place near the Van Loos's, or walking the four blocks to their home. She elected to go on foot.

Moving rapidly until she came to Captain's Row, Martha crossed the cobblestone street gingerly, stepping carefully in the dusky darkness. No one was sure whether the rounded, melon-size stones had come to Alexandria as ballast in sailing ships or been dredged from the Potomac. Tradition had it that Hessian prisoners had been

16

forced to lay them during the Revolution. As a lifelong Alexandria resident, Martha knew they were jarring to the few cars that ventured onto the street and treacherous for high heels. She crossed to her friend's house, glad to reach the smoother brick sidewalk and the freshly painted wooden door.

The front of the Van Loos house had the cherished look of a good restoration, the brass knocker gleaming under the yellow light of a lantern. Flush to the sidewalk, as all the town's mid-Georgian and federal-style homes were, the house was only two stories but was larger than the Graves's row house. All the windows glowed invitingly through filmy curtains, and she could see people congregated in the front room.

John Van Loos greeted her at the door, kissing her on the forehead, as he usually did. Ten years older than Rhonda, he was prematurely bald but the quiet good humor on his face made him an attractive man. Martha was fond of him and never questioned her friend's judgment in marrying a divorced man with three children entering their teens. Rhonda enjoyed her stepchildren's twice-monthly visits but didn't seem to harbor the slightest interest in becoming a mother herself. It was the one thing about her that Martha found puzzling. If, by some miracle, she ever did meet a man she could love wholeheartedly, she wanted children to share their love.

Where did Rhonda find so many people? Martha wandered through the crowded front room and into the dining area where the table had been pushed against one wall. There wasn't a single familiar face, and the host and hostess were nowhere in sight.

Remembering how hungry she was, she surveyed the table, spread with a feast of cheese and crackers. Because of her husband's business and the samples he brought home, Rhonda never used china if paper would serve. Martha picked up a paper plate decorated with yellow alligators.

"There's not a bite to eat or drink on this table that hasn't crossed an ocean."

The male voice directly behind her was so self-assured and cocky, she automatically wanted to refute the claim. A hasty glance at the cheese arranged on small alligator plates told her she didn't have an argument. Her professional eye recognized John's favorite Mascarpone from Italy and mildly spiced Norwegian Nokkelost with its waxy red covering. The French Brie beside a heap of Norwegian flatbread was half gone, and at the far end, German Moselle and French Burgundy sat beside Portuguese wine from Madeira and her favorite sweet wine, fruity Amontillado from Spain.

"I guess these people haven't discovered Wisconsin cheese or California wine," the man said, stepping up to the table beside her.

"It's a lovely assortment," Martha said defensively, looking into a swarthy face with Grecian features.

"But it's not doing our balance of trade any good."

Maybe John and Rhonda did overdo on foreign delicacies, Martha thought, but she resented criticism from this stranger whose dark eyes met hers with unblinking directness, forcing her to look away first. Her fleeting impression was that he was too handsome to appeal to her; his patrician nose, prominent cheekbones, and strong square chin were almost a model of male beauty. Then she looked again and noticed his flaws: brows too thick and close together, a fine white scar on the side of his chin, and tiny wrinkles creasing the corners of his eyes. Somehow the imperfections added to his attractiveness, just as a light sprinkling of white hair among the coal

18

black added dignity and promised he'd someday have beautiful salt and pepper hair which would gradually turn to silvery elegance. Still, he irritated her.

"Don't you approve of sampling what the rest of the world has to offer?"

She immediately regretted her challenge, sure that it sounded snobbish, but the man was insufferable. There were dozens of ways to start a conversation at a party, but knocking the host's refreshments was the worst.

"I do, when it means triple-crème cheese."

He reached for a plain unsalted cracker, the choice of a knowledgeable gourmet, and spread creamy white cheese on it, moving it to her lips in one fluid gesture.

"Taste it," he urged, letting his finger caress the corner of her mouth.

The cracker touched her lips, coating the upper one with the silky-smooth spread, leaving her little choice but to bite off a small portion. The cheese was sinfully rich, so delicious she couldn't resist holding it on her tongue for a moment.

"Triple-crème has to be seventy-five percent butterfat," the stranger said. "It's a French law."

"It's delicious," she was forced to admit.

"I think they invented it for silky lips like yours." His grin was teasing but his eyes were seductive, holding Martha's gaze when she would've been much more comfortable escaping from him.

"Let me choose your wine," he said walking to the array of opened bottles.

The Van Loos were certainly letting their guests shift for themselves tonight, Martha thought, not spotting them anywhere. She started to protest, not liking the dark-haired man's compliment or his courtliness, because he was showering them on a stranger. She had a theory

19

that good friendships ripened like superb cheeses: slowly, under ideal, controlled conditions.

"Something sweet with the triple-crème," he said, handing her a half-filled goblet. "Amontillado, because I like the name. I'd like to know your name."

"Thank you," she said stiffly, accepting the crystal goblet, glad that John refused to let Rhonda serve wine in plastic cups even if his company did sell billions of them.

The stranger poured a second portion for himself and raised his glass to hers. "Cheers?"

His left brow arched, but what she noticed were his lashes, thick and long over a gaze that was too perceptive. Did he know he was making her uneasy? Was he doing it on purpose? Maybe that was his technique with women: make an outrageous statement, then sow confusion by being gallant and chivalrous. She was too busy trying to fathom his game to enjoy the fruity taste of the wine. When he prepared a second cracker with triple-crème and handed it to her, she accepted with a curt "Thanks."

"You finally got here! What took you so long?"

Rhonda swooped down, resplendent in a shiny green and gold floral-patterned, floor-length hostess gown with great batwing sleeves. It made Martha feel like a common bluebird in the company of a peacock, but Rhonda's elaborate gown wasn't what annoyed her. After rushing to the party, she didn't appreciate being accused of tardiness by a hostess who hid from her guests.

"Where've *you* been?" Martha countered.

"Randy broke his arm playing something or other. My stepson," she said, smiling at the man who was still standing nearby. "We had a four-phone call going, and of course, all the kids wanted to tell their dad a different version. You know how a domestic crisis can be, Greg."

"Afraid I don't." He looked at Martha. "I've never had time to get married."

"Greg." Rhonda took his arm possessively; even in heels she was a little shorter than him, which meant he was at least six feet tall. "This is Martha Graves, our favorite cookbook author. I showed you all her wonderful books. I love *The Colonial Wives' Treasury,* and *The Hot Hearth Handbook.* In fact, I love all of them."

Martha was proud of her output, but most of her books were pamphlets; the new full-sized ones were hardly overflowing Rhonda's shelves. She was used to her friend's enthusiastic introductions but usually Rhonda was matchmaking, not promoting cookbooks.

"Martha, this is Gregory Kent."

"Mr. Kent." She nodded her head, hanging onto her wine in her right hand. He set his on the table and took her left hand in his, squeezing it gently and managing to caress her inner wrist with his little finger before he let go.

"Greg," he corrected. "I thought you might be Martha Graves. I saw a little of your television show last time I was in the area. John made a point of telling me not to miss it."

"Oh?" Even though she'd been a guest on a local talk show numerous times, demonstrating how to prepare colonial dishes, it always surprised her that someone besides her mother actually watched TV at nine in the morning.

"Greg's spending the weekend with us," Rhonda said, letting Martha know the reason for the last-minute party. "He's the president and owner of all those Turkey Haven restaurants; you know, the chain that serves turkey twenty tasty ways."

21

"I don't own them all outright. Some are franchises," he said.

Martha was glad Rhonda's extravagant introduction didn't particularly please him either. What was she cooking up this time?

"Well, it's been nice meeting you." Martha put the half-filled goblet on the table and backed away, but Rhonda wasn't going to let her escape that easily.

"People are starting to leave already. John made a ten o'clock dinner reservation for four. You will join us, won't you, Martha?"

"You didn't say anything about dinner on the phone," Martha said sweetly, fuming inwardly at her friend's audacity; she had this blind date all planned. How could she be so sneaky?

"It must've slipped my mind. But you don't have other plans, do you?"

Usually her friend's high-handedness only aroused an amused tolerance in Martha, but tonight she was annoyed as Mr. What's-His-Name beamed a know-it-all smile at her, as though he enjoyed watching Rhonda trying to outmaneuver her.

"I really do." She planned to slip away from the bridge players as quickly as possible, cuddle up in her old green fleece robe, and munch on a cold roast beef sandwich while she started reading what could be a treasure cache of genuine colonial era recipes. "In fact, I should be leaving right now. Nice to have met you, Mr. . . ."

"Kent," Rhonda said quickly.

"Greg," he insisted. "Do you have a car with you?"

"No, I live too close to bother."

"I'll walk you home then."

"No, really—"

"That's a wonderful idea," Rhonda interrupted. "You

22

two have so much in common—food and all. Greg's gotten millions of people to eat turkey and drink out of John's cups."

Martha couldn't believe her friend had said that! Whatever'd happened to subtlety and finesse, the basic tools of the matchmaker's trade? Rhonda's pseudo-oriental gown made her look like a peacock; Martha had an awful urge to pluck some tail feathers!

"No, I wouldn't dream of stealing your guest, Rhonda," Martha insisted.

"Oh, John and Greg are old friends, just like you and me. We see him often, but not as often as we'd like."

Martha barely managed to surpress a "humbug!" Wait until Rhonda wanted her to stand all day in drizzling rain to bid on painted commodes and boxes of spinning wheel parts. Friendship bestowed only so many privileges!

"Did you wear a coat?" Greg asked.

"Yes, but you don't need to bother."

"I don't want you to walk home alone at night."

She wanted to point out that she'd arrived alone after dark but decided it was pointless.

"I'll get my coat. Thank you John, Rhonda."

By the time she found her belted navy coat in the heap in John's office, Greg was behind her, helping her into it, resting his hand on her shoulder for a moment before pulling on his own camel's hair topcoat. She liked his clothes: a dark charcoal suit with a faint pattern of red lines, a brilliantly white shirt with a stiffly starched collar, and a precisely knotted deep red silk tie. He was a man she'd look at twice in any crowd; in fact, she was going to have a hard time getting the spicy scent of his aftershave out of her nostrils.

23

"Do you live with anyone?" he asked when they were alone outside on the brick sidewalk.

"My mother," she said tersely.

He touched her arm, an alarming gesture even though she'd expected it. Since the first moment she'd looked into his face, the message there had been plain: he wanted to seduce her. Was she becoming an hysterical old maid, the kind of woman who'd talked to cats and brewed love potions in colonial days? When he moved his hand from her elbow to her shoulder, sliding his fingers under the curling mane of hair on her neck, she knew she wasn't imagining his intentions. Gregory Kent moved too fast for her.

The night was clear, and the moonlight gave the cobblestone street a fairy-tale quality. In her haste to get home, Martha leaped from stone to stone, forcing her escort to drop his arm and pay attention to his own footing. She was a foot from the brick pavement edging the far side of the street when a cracking noise sent her tumbling forward, landing on both knees. Her heel, caught between two cobblestones, snapped off completely.

Tears of anger filled her eyes even before she knew whether she was hurt. Then his arms were around her and soft words caressed her ear, adding confusion to her embarrassment and humiliation.

"Are you hurt?" he asked for the third time, finally forcing her to respond.

"I broke my heel." She choked back her sobs, feeling like an absolute idiot.

"But are you hurt?" He helped her to stand, holding her upright against his side.

"No, no, I don't think so."

Her knees smarted, and when she looked down she saw that her hose was tattered and her knees were scraped. A little pain she could handle; making a fool of herself was far worse.

"What an idiotic street!" he said harshly.

"It's very historical!"

"So are stocks and whipping posts, but I don't see any around today."

"That's not the same thing at all!"

"A menace is a menace. Let me carry you back to John's, and I'll drive you home in his car. This infernal street isn't even safe for cars!"

"You wouldn't rip up a two-hundred-year-old cobblestone street just because someone might fall, would you?" Her legs were trembling but shock at his attitude made her forget the pain in her knees.

"Someone did fall—you. I wouldn't put history ahead of public safety. Put your arms around my neck."

"I can walk!" She took a shaky step toward the brick paving, limping on the heelless shoe.

"Here's your heel. Maybe it can be fixed."

"Thank you." She stuffed it into her pocket, sure that it couldn't be nailed back on to her shoe.

"Let me help you," he insisted.

"I don't need help, thank you."

She only wished he hadn't seen her fall!

"At least take my arm."

He sounded so unhappy, she hooked her arm in his, surprised at how strong his arm felt through both of their heavy coat sleeves. They walked in silence for a full block, Martha walking on one tiptoe rather than bouncing along on the broken heel.

"You didn't need to run away from me," he said at last, speaking so softly she had to strain to catch his words.

"I wasn't!" she protested vehemently.

"No? Then you must expect stone-hopping to become an Olympic sport."

There was nothing she could answer, and this made her furious. Gregory Kent might be the turkey king of the world, but he was too much for her—too self-assured, too all-knowing, and even too handsome. She wanted a shy man with big ears and a small ego, not an aggressive fast-talking manipulator who stripped her naked with his eyes.

At the alleyway she stopped to unlock the gate, intending to close the iron barrier between them, but he anticipated her evasiveness, stepping into the narrow passageway before she could shut it.

"My mother has guests. I'll just slip in the back way."

"Rhonda said your mother was in a serious accident."

"Yes, but she's doing fine now."

"I understand she had extensive surgery."

"Yes, she was in the operating room nearly seven hours after the accident. There was a chance she'd lose the use of one leg."

She didn't tell him the cost of that surgery was threatening to ruin them; their insurance company said the doctor's charges were neither "reasonable nor customary." They could be left thousands of dollars in debt.

"I'll be staying with John and Rhonda this weekend. I'd like to see you again."

"No, I don't think so, Greg. Thank you for asking."

Her key was in her hand and the kitchen door was open before he could respond to her decision.

"Thank you for walking me home," she added.

"You would've been safer alone, I guess." He laughed lightly, an altogether pleasant sound that made her even more anxious to get away from him.

"The gate opens from this side without a key. It will lock if you pull it tightly shut."

"I'll be sure you're locked in for the night," he said with mock gravity.

The bridge players were in the middle of a slam bid. It was the best luck she'd had all evening; her mother hardly noticed her limp past to the stairs and her room.

Later, dressed for bed with a cold washcloth on one black and blue knee, she was fuming angrily about the call that had summoned her to Rhonda's party. She remembered fragments of conversation with her friend and with her mother. Wasn't there supposed to be a financial reason for meeting Gregory Kent? Certainly nothing at all businesslike came up in the conversation she had with him. Rhonda must have invented it as an excuse for yet another matchmaking attempt. Their friendship had never been on shakier ground!

Even if there was a good reason for meeting the turkey tycoon, Martha couldn't imagine going along with anything he suggested. He had the kind of energy that swept people into his orbit; he was used to doing things his way and having people fall into step with him. Gregory Kent was simply more man than she wanted to tangle with.

Sitting on her window seat an hour later, she saw her mother's guests leave and shortly afterward heard the door of the second-floor bedroom close. She should've helped her mother up the stairs so the seat of her velvet dress wouldn't get ruined, Martha thought. It was too late, and this was one of the rare occasions when she didn't welcome her mother's friendly companionship. She had nothing to share with Fleury tonight.

When she finally went to bed, she lay imagining the taste of rich French cheese and the touch of a strong

27

finger caressing the corner of her mouth. In her fantasy, she drew the finger between her lips and rolled it over her tongue, finding it sweeter than ripe peaches and smoother than pure cream.

CHAPTER TWO

"I've been reading the insurance policy again and everything Mr. Houston told us is right here. They don't have to pay the whole bill if the doctor overcharges." Fleury frowned at a sheath of papers.

"That's the twentieth time you've read it!" Martha poured a cup of coffee and joined her mother at the old gateleg table in the kitchen, sorry she'd wasted half the morning by sleeping late. "He's been our agent for years. We'll just have to see what he says when we meet with him next week."

"I suppose so. I feel so helpless. If I could earn some money—"

"Your benefits pay more than your share of our expenses, Mother," Martha responded automatically. They'd had this conversation many times before and it was impossible to convince Fleury that she wasn't a burden.

"They'll run out soon. I do have an idea." Her voice perked up. "Lydia says there's a tremendous demand for free-lance typists. I'm sure I could work a few hours a day at home, if you don't mind me using your typewriter."

"I don't mind if you use it, but not until the doctor says it's okay."

"What could it hurt if I type a few business reports or maybe a term paper or two?"

"Or a doctoral thesis or a novel? Mom, you won't do either of us any good if you overdo now."

"I've been so worried about what I can do to help, I forgot to ask about your advance on the Sugar Glen cookbook."

Martha sipped her coffee and tried to think of a way to break the bad news.

"I agreed to do the book. They have a wonderful hoard of old receipts." After years of research she used the old fashioned word for recipes without thinking about it. "But the society is nearly broke from restoring the Silas Strucker house."

"No advance?" her mother asked, trying to hide her disappointment.

"A token, but they went up two percentage points on the royalty."

"Why couldn't I have an accident close to home? Dr. Feister never overcharges like that Baltimore doctor."

"A G.P. doesn't do bone surgery."

Martha grinned at her mother, and they both laughed, because it kept them from crying.

"So, what was Rhonda's big surprise?"

"She wanted me to meet someone—as usual."

"That's all?"

Martha shrugged. "I really don't know. I left early."

"Was he that bad?" Fleury pursed her lips skeptically.

"It would be much easier on all of us if Rhonda would start fixing you up!"

"I wouldn't waste her time. Men my age are looking for women your age. You couldn't have gotten very well acquainted in the short time you were gone. Was he terribly unattractive?"

30

"He was tall, dark, and handsome. Charming, articulate, poised, and sexy."

"Ah!"

"Ah, what?"

"Just ah. I wish . . ."

"What?" Martha got up to drop a slice of bread into the toaster.

"Never mind."

Fleury knocked over one of her stout metal crutches, and Martha picked it up.

"You wish I hadn't waited all those years for Peter to get the peace corps out of his system."

"Which he never did do."

"But it didn't matter, because we decided there was no future for us."

"How could there be a future when he was chasing after that skinny girl from South Carolina?"

"Please, Mother, not before breakfast!"

The phone on the kitchen counter rang shrilly, and Martha grabbed it up on the second ring.

"Miss Graves?" The man's voice was full and throaty, with bell-clear tones and the relaxed pronunciation of a midwesterner. She had to be imagining the little tingle at the base of her spine.

"Yes."

"Greg Kent. We met last night."

"Yes, I remember." She could almost feel the buttery smoothness of triple-crème cheese on her tongue.

"I realize you're busy, but it's important I see you again this weekend."

"I do have plans. . . ."

Hearing his voice this morning, she was having a hard time remembering why she'd been so eager to avoid him.

"I have a business offer for you. Rhonda and John thought you might be interested."

"What sort of offer?" She tried to keep her raging curiosity out of her voice.

"I'm in the process of planning a new line of restaurants with a colonial-American theme. I may have some work for you."

"I see."

She didn't have the vaguest idea what she might do for a restaurant chain but he certainly had her attention.

"I have to be on a plane to Chicago tomorrow noon. We can get together any time between now and then. Just tell me when."

"I could meet you in an hour or so, I suppose." Worried that she sounded too eager, she added, "For just a short time."

"Fine, I'll pick you up in one hour."

"He says he has a business offer for me," Martha said to her mother after replacing the receiver.

"Who's he?"

"Gregory Kent, the man I met last night. I think he buys a lot of containers from John for his Turkey Havens."

"He's the tall, dark, and handsome one?" her mother teased.

"Not to mention pushy and egotistical!"

"Umm. Your toast is getting cold."

"Save it for the bird feeder. I have to get dressed."

Fleury settled herself on a corner of the couch, the surgical scars on her leg concealed by her lilac satin robe. She didn't comment when Martha came downstairs in wine-colored jeans and a bulky-knit beige sweater, walking a little stiffly from her tumble on the cobblestones.

"If he does have a job offer, I'll be glad to help with the Sugar Glen cookbook," her mother suggested.

"You'll be my number-one taster, as always," Martha said, gently refusing her mother's help.

She never adapted an old recipe for modern use without experimenting first, and hoped many of the Sugar Glen recipes were variations of familiar ones, so she wouldn't have to prepare every dish included in the new book. Culinary experiments were expensive!

The door buzzer had been installed by Grandfather Graves when he remodeled the house in 1928. Martha intended to dispense with its annoying sound before it became an antique. Nothing would please her more than to rely on a door knocker the way the original owners of the house had.

Hatless with the wind whipping his hair away from his forehead, Gregory Kent reminded Martha of a poem she'd once read about a "bonnie" highwayman. The air was cold, but he wasn't wearing a coat over his gray tweed sport jacket and black turtleneck. His chin above the high, rolled collar was lean and square. He had to be thirty-five but he walked past her into the living room with the athletic briskness of a man ten years younger.

Martha introduced him to her mother but was anxious to leave because her curiosity was getting the better of her. What did this man want with her?

Greg sat on a small chair opposite her mother, pulling it closer and leaning forward to respond to Fleury.

"Mr. Kent, it's such a pleasure to meet you. Have you known John and Rhonda very long?"

"John and I were friends in college."

"Let me see, John went somewhere in the Midwest, didn't he?"

33

"He got his undergraduate degree from Michigan State University."

"Oh, so that's where you graduated too?"

Martha didn't sit. She knew her mother was bored with her confinement and welcomed company, but hoped her interrogation would be short.

"No, ma'am." He said ma'am as though it were an unfamiliar courtesy; Fleury did strike people as a ladylike Southern belle even though she'd grown up in a small town in Rhode Island. "I learned all I needed to know in two and a half years, so I quit."

"To go into the restaurant business?" Fleury managed to conceal disapproval of his attitude toward higher education.

"I was already in it. I had a pizza place in East Lansing."

"Oh, your family was in the restaurant. . . ."

"I think Greg and I had better be going, Mother," Martha interrupted.

Greg stood but didn't follow when she moved to the door. "No, they ran a neighborhood grocery store in Chicago. They're retired in Florida now."

"But didn't you want to get your degree?"

Fleury tried not to sound shocked; her own degree in French literature had nothing to do with her career as a legal secretary, but she treasured it.

"Degrees look good on resumés," he said, "but I never planned to fill one out."

"Oh, you never planned to work for anyone but yourself," Fleury said, sounding a little floored.

"I never have." He took her hand, squeezed it lightly and smiled winningly. "It's been a pleasure meeting you, Mrs. Graves."

34

Fleury literally beamed at him, his lack of a degree forgotten.

Martha was annoyed but she didn't like herself for feeling that way. She wanted her mother to like her friends, but Greg wasn't a friend. Until he gave her a reason to consider him differently, she saw him as an adversary. Having her mother in his cheering section was definitely irritating.

"Your mother is delightful," he said when they were outside. "Does she still have a lot of pain?"

It was the one question that could make her warm to him. Most people didn't suspect that under Fleury's fluffy exterior there was the iron will of a stoic.

"Quite a bit, but she's learning to cope without medication. She won't admit it when she is suffering."

He'd borrowed John's New Yorker and parked it in front of her house, reminding her that the Honda was still three blocks away. By the time she took care of a pileup of household jobs, she'd be lucky to get at the Sugar Glen receipts by late afternoon. Greg touched her elbow to guide her to the car, seating her with practiced smoothness.

Getting behind the wheel, he turned a devastating smile on her, but she reacted with suspicion. What did this man want from her?

"I thought we could drive awhile, see a little of the countryside," he suggested.

"I'm really sorry but I'm terribly short of time right now. I spent all of yesterday at Sugar Glen and I'm just starting a new project."

Her protests sounded a little halfhearted; he was the most attractive man she'd met in a long time.

"I hope you're not too busy to do some work for me."

"You haven't told me what you have in mind yet."

35

"John and Rhonda had to go out for a while. Why don't we drive over to their place, and I'll lay it out for you?"

"Couldn't you just ask me here?"

"All right." He sounded like a person whose suggestions were usually followed. "I'm in the planning stages of a new line of franchises but I want to get away from the fast food take-out line. What I have in mind is a colonial family-style restaurant. I want you to help develop the menu."

"Based on colonial cookery?" She was intrigued in spite of her misgivings about him.

"Exactly."

"I don't know anything about food preparation in modern restaurants."

"I have people for that." He started the car. "What I need from you is the authentic touch. Let's go over to John's, and I'll show you some of the preliminary plans."

Rhonda was better at setting up parties than cleaning up afterward. The front room was stale with the smell of unemptied ashtrays, and remnants of cheese were drying out on paper plates, looking less appetizing than the yellow alligators.

"The plans are up in the guest room I'm using." Greg took her coat and laid it over an arm of the silver and green striped Empire sofa, one of the many lovely period pieces Rhonda had found while working with her aunt. "Come on up."

"Why don't you bring them down to John's office? You can spread them out on his library table."

So far today Greg had been all business—except when he was charming her mother into girlish giggles. Deciding what to do about his offer would be difficult enough without holding a conference on Rhonda's four-poster guest bed.

"If that's what you want."

He looked at her again the way he had last night at the cheese table, making her aware of the generous swell of her breasts under the heavy sweater. Hoping that her face wasn't as red as it was warm, she walked through the hallway to the closed door of John's office, waiting there until he returned with several long rolls of paper.

"These are only tentative blueprints," he explained, rolling one out on the mahogany table in the center of the room. "I plan to pinpoint medium-size towns with large universities, not so much for student trade as all the visitors they attract for other events: athletics, conferences, that sort of business."

The architect's drawing of the interior didn't mean much to her, other than to show that the kitchen seemed small in proportion to the seating space for diners.

"This will give you a better idea."

He unrolled a colored drawing of the facade of a restaurant. Except for a pair of white columns by the entrance, it didn't look much different from a thousand other family-type eating places.

He leaned over to anchor the corners with a glass paperweight from Niagara Falls and an old pearl-handled letter opener with British Guiana engraved on the blade, then turned to her expectantly. She didn't know quite how to react.

"The columns will be a hallmark, like orange-tiled roofs or golden arches," he said.

"I see. Will they be wooden?"

"No." He laughed. "We're looking at hollow metal."

There wasn't anything she could say to that.

37

"If you're busy all day, why don't we have a late dinner? There's a lot to discuss," he said.

"I'm not sure if—"

"Don't say yes or no now. At least give me a chance to convince you."

She met his eyes for the first time that day, realizing that she'd been avoiding his direct gaze. Did she want to be convinced to work for him? It was hard to look at his dark eyes and react in a negative way. After all, what did she have to lose by listening? She'd never needed extra work more urgently.

"I could be free later this evening," she said in a tentative voice.

"Wonderful! Is eight o'clock too early?"

"No, that will be fine, but I have to go now. I'll walk because I have to pick up my car. Our alley was blocked last night, so I had to park a few blocks away." She spilled out these words so fast she felt breathless, needing a gulp of fresh river air to clear her head.

Out on the street she felt as though she'd just raced up six flights of steps. Her pulse was hammering in her forehead and she stepped over the cobblestones with exaggerated caution, only too well aware that she was being watched from the open door of the Van Loos house. All the man had offered was a one-shot assignment, the chance to do some menu research and adapt it to modern usage. She did that sort of thing for a living, although never before for such a commercial purpose. There was no reason to feel so flustered and flattered and threatened, she reminded herself.

Out of his sight, she walked rapidly, wondering why he was using so much charm to get her to work for him. If his offer was a good one, she couldn't afford to refuse. Did she have it in her to say no to anything he suggested?

His brash self-assurance made her want to thwart him, but every once in a while there was a flash of something else, a tenderness under the self-assertive veneer.

She was imagining things! With a man as handsome as Greg, it was easy to believe he was noble in a sort of poetic way. Her only real worry was that he'd charm her into doing something she really didn't want to tackle.

Throwing open both doors of the wardrobe cupboard that compensated for the absence of closets in the house, Martha surveyed the contents, realizing for the first time that half of everything she owned was blue: navy, sky, aquamarine, or Wedgwood. She was in a rut and her clothing was proof of it. Her mood demanded something vibrant and dashing, something to make her look more exciting and confident than she felt. Even Rhonda's peacock dress would be an improvement over the drab contents of her wardrobe!

Deliberately kicking off her noisy mules, she crept barefoot down one flight of stairs. Before the accident her mother had sometimes worn the same size as Martha; she loved clothes and had two full wardrobes to her daughter's one. Fleury would willingly loan anything she owned but she'd also tease her daughter about a sudden interest in dressing up.

Most of the dresses were much too short, but Martha found one she hardly remembered her mother wearing. The dress was a deep burgundy sheath with dolman sleeves. It just might be long enough!

Martha tried it first, then asked her mother if she could wear it. At the last minute she nearly changed her mind. The rayon jersey accentuated her curves, making her breasts seem full and provocative. The material clung to her bottom and thighs even after she sprayed the skirt

39

with an anti-static compound. The dress didn't look too small, but she felt as if there was too much of her in it. She'd decided to change to a navy suit when the door buzzer sounded. Her mother was comfortably settled on the couch to watch a TV program, so Martha raced down two flights to answer the summons.

"Good evening, Martha."

Why did he make such a commonplace greeting sound so special? She wasn't sure whether to feel flattered or wary.

"Greg." She nodded her head. "I left my purse upstairs. Say hello to Mother, and I'll be right back."

She hurried up the stairs, aware that he was watching her rear. Darn! Now she really did want to change into something more conservative, but it would look silly if she changed clothes now.

With hundreds of restaurants in the Washington, D.C., area within easy reach, he couldn't have picked a more pleasing one. Dimly lit with candles, the series of intimate dining rooms had small tables set with starched white linen and polished silverware. A team of dark-haired waiters with French accents took their dinner orders, brought delicious hard-crust rolls, and filled their water glasses, adding thin slices of fresh lemon. It didn't seem quite real, being served by darkly romantic waiters in black jackets, sitting across from a man who overshadowed the most handsome of them.

They ordered trout almondine; Greg said he rarely ate red meat anymore. The tiny parsley potatoes were so perfect Martha envied the chef's skill.

"This is marvelous," she said, breaking a spear of asparagus with her fork.

"This is the kind of food I want to offer my customers,

40

without the fancy prices: tasty, greaseless, healthy food with good seasonings."

"Health food?" She looked at him thoughtfully.

"Not the seaweed salad, soybean-burger type. Just good ingredients prepared in an appealing way. That's where I hope you can help me. Quite a few authentic recipes call for a lot of good produce: pumpkins, sweet potatoes, black-eyed peas, eggplant, apples."

"You already know about colonial cookery, don't you?"

He looked a little sheepish. "Some."

"I can't understand why you need my help. I don't know anything about restaurants."

"I want your ideas." His voice caressed the word *want*.

"I'm not sure about restaurant techniques."

"My staff can develop feasible procedures. I guess what I want from you is a touch of class. Anybody can serve food. It takes a special knack to create the right aura."

"Aura?"

"That's a gimmick with class. In the Turkey Havens, I've been selling health with economy. Turkey is low-fat and cheaper than beef. Make it taste good, and it's ideal for a fast meal. In the colonial restaurants I want people to know they're not eating a dinner full of chemicals."

"You want people to associate your food with a healthier, simpler life-style?"

"Something like that."

"I don't know what I could contribute. Your experts can get the same thing from some of the better cookbooks on the colonial period."

"No, they don't have your special expertise. I'm willing to pay well for this, Martha." He named an hourly rate that almost made her gasp. "But there's a catch. I'm in a hurry."

41

So were the women of the Sugar Glen Historical Society. She didn't know what to say.

"How much of a hurry?"

"You can't get your ideas to me too soon."

Was his proposal as exciting as it seemed or was she being swayed by his intensity and persuasiveness? Part of her wanted to jump at the opportunity; she might be able to combine it with her research on the Sugar Glen receipts. Her mother would love to help with the preliminary sorting and classifying; it might be good therapy for Fleury.

"What do you think?" he asked softly.

"I'm not sure. You make it sound so simple, but it won't be easy to adapt colonial receipts—recipes—to use in a modern restaurant."

"You modernize all the recipes in your books, don't you?"

"I convert the measurements to cups and tablespoons, that sort of thing. But colonial women spent all day cooking. Most of their dishes are very time-consuming to prepare. I don't want to accept your offer if I can't find what you need."

"If I'm willing to invest money, aren't you willing to invest time?"

His challenge didn't push her into saying yes: on the contrary, it made her even more hesitant. Lurking just below the surface in their conversation was a contest of wills; he was determined to have her go along with his plans, she wasn't at all sure she should.

They ended the meal with a scoop of apricot ice and flaky wafers, then lingered over cups of rich, aromatic coffee.

"As often as I've passed through Washington, I haven't found time to see the Vietnam Memorial," he said when they returned to John's car. "Do you mind if we stop for a look?"

She was in no hurry at all to have the evening end.

Even on this cold night there were visitors paying homage to Abraham Lincoln, little clusters of people awed by the great seated statue of the nation's noblest president. They parked close to this monument and Greg led her up the steps to it, keeping her hand warmly clasped in his. Neither said much; Martha had made pilgrimages to the foot of the statue for as long as she could remember but she still felt a reverent hush at the memory of Lincoln's great love for humanity.

Still silent, they descended and made their way to the long, dark wall commemorating the casualties of the Vietnam war. Unlit at night, the black marble engraved with the names of all the lost men seemed a grim and fitting monument to Martha. She kept quiet, waiting for Greg's reaction.

"My God, so many," he said hoarsely.

He didn't need to say anything else. They walked back to the car hand-in-hand. The long pauses in their conversation on the drive back to her house didn't seem awkward, but she found herself wishing she could read Greg's mind. Until he'd kissed her, their dinner date had been a casual meeting to discuss business.

"I enjoyed myself tonight," he said, breaking the silence and reaching over to caress her hand with his.

"I had a nice time too."

"You haven't told me much about yourself," he said.

"You know the basics—a degree in history, my cookbooks and pamphlets, my mother."

"The only question I consider basic is whether there's a man in your life."

43

"Oh." She sat up straighter, afraid that he'd think less of her if she told him the truth.

"Is there?" he persisted.

"Not right now, no."

She expected him to comment in some way but he lapsed into another long silence.

"There was a man in the peace corps." She felt compelled to mention some love interest, then decided Peter wasn't worth describing at any length. Her mother had built their on-and-off affair into much more than it really was. "Well, that's history."

"Never my best subject."

It was Martha's best subject, so she didn't say anything else.

Again finding a parking place practically in front of her door, he turned off the motor and lights.

"I really do need an answer from you soon." He half turned to face her, but the streetlight was too far down the block for her to see his expression.

"Yes, I understand. I just need a little time to think about it."

"I hope to be back here by the end of the week. I'm looking at some property in the area. Is that enough time to think?" He sounded a little impatient; as a man who made multimillion dollar decisions, he probably didn't understand why she was hesitating.

"That's very fair," she said a little stiffly.

"Is it?" He reached out and placed his fingers under her chin, turning her face toward his.

"I'll do some preliminary research to see if I can come up with anything you can use," she promised.

"Keep track of your hours."

When he sounded so businesslike, she didn't want him to touch her. Quickly getting out of the car, she told herself a good-night kiss was the last thing she wanted from Gregory Kent.

"Let me walk you to the back," he said, following her to the gate.

"It's not necessary."

'Here." He took her key and unlocked the gate with less difficulty than she usually had working the old lock.

Stepping ahead of her into the passageway, he returned the key and let her pull the gate shut, trapping her between the iron bars and his body. Leaning his forearms on the brick walls, he neatly confined her to the narrow bit of space in front of him.

"You're trapped," he teased.

He was right; there wasn't even room to duck under his arms.

"Well, thank you for the dinner." She was trying to convince herself that no friend of John's was a real threat.

"Thank you for your company."

"Are you going to let me pass?"

"Of course. As soon as . . ."

His kiss was playful, teasing her lips apart and toying with them.

"Does your mother wait up for you?"

"Always," Martha lied.

"Never any necking on the couch?"

Anything she said would sound like an invitation. She wasn't at all sure she could handle this aggressive, self-assured man. He was far too used to getting his own way.

He stopped playing with her mouth and kissed her seriously, encircling her with his arms and rubbing his body against hers.

Unbuttoning her coat, he slid his hands under it, warming them on the curve of her hips. The borrowed dress felt slinkier than ever, and she wriggled free, backing up against the gate.

"I won't always have to corner you," he warned softly, turning and leading her down the passageway to the walled garden.

"You won't always have a chance," she quipped before hurrying into the house.

CHAPTER THREE

Fleury was delighted to help with the Sugar Glen recipes; her first job was to decipher some of the hard-to-read handwritten directions on the photocopies. Working on the couch with a lap board, she made legible copies in her own neat printing, complaining because Martha wouldn't let her begin typing them.

"Let's pick the ones to use first, at least one from every member," Martha said, finding it unusually difficult to concentrate on this marvelous hoard of family recipes.

Monday she temporarily abandoned the Sugar Glen project; her mind was too preoccupied with Greg's offer to give the cookbook project her best efforts. Searching her own books and files, she found a way of preparing fried oysters that might fit his requirements.

The next day she made spoonbread for dinner, deciding the hot cornbread might be something Greg could serve. Wednesday she researched vegetables and came up with an eggplant pie but wasn't sure it would appeal to his customers.

It was unreasonable to expect a man as busy as he was to call; he certainly had more important things to do than check on her. Still, she couldn't answer the phone without feeling a twinge of disappointment when it proved to be someone other than Greg.

Thursday she admitted to herself she'd very much like

to see Greg again. Dinner included a sweet potato soufflé she'd added to the collection of recipes she planned to show him.

Surely he'd return on Friday; he'd said the end of the week. She was beginning to feel guilty about delegating so much of the Sugar Glen work to her mother. After an afternoon of classifying the society's recipes, she started facing some of the cookbook problems. A few recipes had apparently been pilfered from books currently in print. Martha knew her field too well to be fooled by a recipe for lemon tea cakes exactly the same as one on page 191 of *The Thirteen Colonies Cookbook*. She made a note on the photocopy and filed it in a folder of rejects. A project like this was sure to cause some hurt feelings and to anger some of the society's members, but they'd hired her to compile a book of original family recipes, not a mishmash of already published ones.

Long after her mother went to bed, she poured over recipes, again abandoning Sugar Glen to work on the menu for Greg. Hogs' ears and cocks' combs were definitely not what he had in mind. She fell asleep and dreamed of serving pigeon pie to a darkly handsome stranger who kept feeling her tidbits with his fingers.

She spent Saturday morning typing a few recipes for Greg. Would the clam soup be too expensive to serve? Was the almond cake too rich? Did he have any intention of coming to Alexandria that weekend?

Using Rhonda's own tactics, she called her friend and learned they were taking John's children to the Space Museum that afternoon. The Van Looses obviously weren't expecting a visitor. Rhonda casually asked whether Martha had accepted Greg's offer, not commenting on her noncommittal answer.

Gregory Kent probably had other interests to fill his

weekends. He wasn't married, but Martha assumed there had to be women in his life, maybe one special woman. Why hadn't she asked when he quizzed her about her love life?

By late afternoon she'd almost convinced herself that seeing him again was a bad idea. They had nothing in common; his life-style, dashing here and there, made her dizzy. Falling in love with a man who was in Chicago one day and Dallas the next could only lead to frustration and disappointment.

Falling in love! Talk about rushing things! She wasn't even sure she liked him!

Her mother's evening was planned; friends were coming for bridge. Martha set up the table and cards before starting an omelet for dinner, wishing her restless, discontented mood would pass. It wasn't like her to brood for no reason; she was much too practical to make herself miserable because the phone didn't ring.

Fleury had graduated to the use of a walking cane that week, limping painfully but pleased by any tangible proof of progress. She insisted on answering the door when her friends arrived, so Martha went to the third floor to make some decisions about cakes and pies. There was a marvelous receipt that called for seven pounds of currants, two pounds of almonds, and two pounds of eggs; it was going to be tricky to cut it down to make one normal-size dessert.

The mirror on her dresser was spotty with age; someday she wanted to have it resilvered. Tonight, by the glow of two small pink-shaded bedroom lamps, it showed a wistful face with large gold-speckled blue eyes and a pug nose that more than one male friend had called cute; nothing annoyed Martha more than having her nose kissed. She'd started life as a towhead but for as long as

49

she could remember, her hair had been several shades, the blond streaks adding liveliness to her features. Regular exercise and cautious eating kept her curves under control; she'd never make it as a model, but considering her fattening profession, her shape was pretty good.

The only full-length mirror in the house was in her mother's room, and it'd been years since she'd paraded nude in front of it, privately assessing how she might look to someone else, to a lover. Running her hand down her sides now, over a slender waist and hips that swelled under old jeans, she knew most men found her attractive but not stunning. No wonder a man like Gregory Kent didn't rush back to Alexandria; he certainly wasn't awestruck by her ravishing beauty or bedazzled by her voluptuous body. He probably only kissed her because she was handy.

Just thinking about him made her tense and edgy. The longer she dawdled over thoughts of him, the more angry she became with herself. The only thing to do was get his address from Rhonda, mail the recipes she'd decided might fit his purposes, and forget him. She didn't want another man popping in and out of her life the way Peter had, especially not one who said he'd come and didn't.

The grating sound of the door buzzer carried faintly to the third floor, and Martha took it as a signal to stop moping over a man she hardly knew. Her mother's friends were there and she had a whole evening to work uninterrupted.

"Martha!"

She heard her mother call but decided, for once, not to respond. The bridge players could get along beautifully without a greeting from her. Walking to her desk she turned on the powerful light sitting there and adjusted the gooseneck so it was shining on a pile of recipes. A knock on her open door made her jump.

"Sorry I startled you." Greg's head nearly touched the top of the low door frame. "Your mother said to come up. She said you were staying in to work tonight."

What kind of mother would send a man like Greg to her daughter's bedroom? Martha decided Rhonda wasn't the worst matchmaker she knew!

"I didn't hear you on the stairs." She cursed herself for sounding so inane; where were her witty quips when she needed them?

"I have a cab waiting. How fast can you get into a party dress?" he asked, smiling.

"I can't think of any reason why I'd want to do that."

"I should've called but it seemed quicker to get a cab and come right here. Your mother said you're a good sport about last minute plans."

Her mother would!

"Greg, I really don't think—"

"The plane sat on the ground in Chicago for an hour waiting to take off or I wouldn't be running so late. Congressman Hailey is expecting us at his party."

"Us? He couldn't possibly be expecting me!"

"I told you I'd be back this weekend."

"You said something about the end of the week, but—"

"We have to get to Georgetown. I'll talk to your mother while you get ready."

"I'm not . . ."

He dashed down the stairs so noisily she was sure he'd deliberately sneaked up.

". . . going!"

He didn't hear; she'd have to follow him downstairs and tell him she couldn't be bulldozed into spending the evening with him. Halfway down the lower flight of stairs she met her mother, who was inching her way upward with a knee that still didn't bend properly.

"Mother, what—"

"Wear my violet sheath, the jersey with the cowl collar," she whispered urgently.

"That's much too short!"

"No, I saw a fashion show on TV. All the best designers are showing some hems above the knees this year." Still hissing the words in a low voice, she added, "it has a designer label. I bought it at a secondhand boutique for more than I ever pay for an ordinary new dress."

The door buzzer sounded, but Martha couldn't get past her mother to answer it. Fleury blocked her way and slowly descended to go to the door herself.

"I'm not going!" Martha called after her mother in a stage whisper.

"Don't be silly!" Her mother didn't lower her voice this time.

Retreating to the second floor while her mother's bridge-playing friends trekked into the lower hallway, Martha didn't know whether to be angrier at her mother or Greg. She had a right to plan her own evening! Now, in order to get rid of him, she had to do it in front of three avidly curious bridge players!

Blaming her racing pulse on being trapped, she angrily sorted through one and then the other of Fleury's wardrobes, pulling out the dress. Her mother had bought it for an anniversary celebration when her father was still alive; Martha remembered loving the deep violet shade, so like the pansies her grandmother used to plant every spring along the walk to her bungalow in Rhode Island. Fleury had never offered to let her wear it before; if she was that

52

susceptible to Greg's charms, she was the one who should be looking for a man!

Rather ashamed of her crossness, Martha carried the dress to her own room. She'd known when she moved home after having her own apartment for two years that there'd be times like this. She didn't like being railroaded into things, not even an evening with a dark, handsome man.

Instead of the shuffle and slap of cards, Martha heard laughter and animated conversation as she came down the stairs dressed again in her mother's clothing, including her favorite jacket—a short black fake fur. Greg was entertaining the four women, who apparently had forgotten they were there to play bridge.

"I'm ready," she said.

Not even her mother noticed that she didn't even say hello.

"We could take my car," she said, sounding a little surly as they left the house.

"I already hired a cab. It's not much of a chariot, but it's ours for the evening."

"Which will be short," she said.

"You're mad." He didn't sound at all disturbed about it.

"I'm not exactly happy! People usually ask me if I want to go out."

"Next time I'll give you a week's notice. I promise." He opened the door of the taxi for her then hurried around to get in on the other side.

Next time! He said it so matter-of-factly. Did he see something that the cloudy mirror over her dresser didn't reveal? Why had he come for her tonight? They didn't have any business that couldn't be handled by a short phone call.

53

"We're going to a party?" she asked to cover her growing agitation.

"We'll make an appearance. I'll try to get away as soon as possible. Bill Hailey is an old friend."

An attendant in a starched white jacket took their coats in an entry hall graced by an Empire sideboard holding a sterling tea service and a pair of candlesticks. With his hand on her waist, Greg guided her into a room the size of a small ballroom filled with French provincial furniture and noisy clusters of people. Heavy emerald-green velvet drapes shut out the outside world. Martha couldn't quite believe she was there. There were several familiar faces she recognized from newspaper photos, and Martha knew her descriptions of the women's gowns would keep her mother entertained for a month.

"Bill, a friend of mine, Martha Graves."

"Martha, what a pleasure to have you here. I can't imagine what Greg's done to deserve such a ravishing companion."

She knew Greg's friend was a politician but his charm was still impressive. She couldn't possibly bring herself to vote against him if he ran in her district but his appearance was nondescript compared to Greg's.

To her surprise people talked to her, seemingly fascinated when she mentioned her occupation. She was having so much fun she almost forgot the host was a well-known congressman. Greg didn't leave her side for more than a minute, instead hovering close, resting his hand on her arm, lacing his fingers through hers. He was wearing a well-tailored charcoal-gray suit. Again his shirt was gleaming white, and his tie deep maroon with narrow black stripes. Women seemed to make a point of speaking to him and he rewarded each and every one with a smile that began to annoy her. He wasn't running for public office!

"Come'ere," he said softly, taking her hand and leading her toward a door at the far end of the crowded room. "There's something I want to show you."

He seemed to know the house well, guiding her through a back hallway to a narrow flight of stairs adjacent to the kitchen.

"Where do these go?" she asked, a little wary of the dark stairway.

"To the servants' quarters. This house was built when the help still lived in."

The bare board steps were steep, and the dim light from below disappeared when they rounded a sharp curve onto a second floor landing.

"I don't see—" she began.

"Neither does anyone else."

He took her in his arms and slowly kissed her. She inhaled a scent so enticing and yet so masculine she felt a little lightheaded.

"I wanted to show you how much I missed you. I've been thinking about you all week." He held her against him, nuzzling the fine, wispy hair that touched her forehead.

"I did some work on the menu."

He didn't seem to care, running his lips back and forth across hers.

"You look beautiful in that dress," he said softly.

His hands slid to rest on her lower back and she tensed her buttocks, anticipating a squeeze that didn't come. He hesitated for a long moment then covered her mouth with his, making her tingle almost unbearably.

"The party . . ."

"I can't go back right now." He laughed softly and released her. "Tell me what you did this week."

For a moment she couldn't remember. "I worked."

"For me?"

"A little. I have a few recipes."

"I have another idea."

"What?"

"I'll tell you later."

Below them electrified lanterns in the courtyard sent just enough light through a small window on the landing for her to see his profile. She wanted to run her finger along his jawbone and rain tiny kisses on the little scar she remembered seeing there.

"How did you cut your chin?"

"My chin?"

"The scar."

"Oh." He touched it as he laughed. "I'd almost forgotten it. A little hassle in the old neighborhood. We lived above the grocery store."

"A fight?"

"Not exactly." He sounded evasive.

"I shouldn't have asked."

"It doesn't matter. I was mugged by three older kids. Lost lunch money and my lucky Chicago Cubs medal. It was the first and only time anyone took anything away from me—and the last time I relied on luck."

She felt as if he'd revealed something important about himself and a little shiver ran down her spine.

"It's a little spooky here."

This time he laughed with genuine amusement. "Don't tell me you're a girl who sees ghosts and goblins everytime the lights go out."

"Hardly!" She was offended at being called a girl.

"Or maybe you're not a girl at all." He ran his fingers

56

over the side of her cheek then brushed them against her lips. "Maybe you're more woman than you realize."

"We'd better go downstairs."

He laughed again, a low chuckle which disturbed her. "Let me go first. These steps are treacherous."

Not as treacherous as the man who'd led her up them, she suspected, resolving to avoid dark landings and unlit corners when she was with Greg. He was much more dangerous than any ghost she was likely to see!

Greg made a smooth exit, making it sound urgent that they leave immediately, without actually giving a reason for departing early.

"Where would you like to go now?" he asked, taking her arm as they stood on the pavement outside.

"Where's your taxi? I thought you hired it for the evening."

"I told the driver ten o'clock. He probably had to park a ways away."

"More likely he's picking up some extra fares on your time."

"I wouldn't think much of his business acumen if he didn't."

"You expect him to be dishonest?"

"I only expect him to live up to the agreement he made with me. Here he is now."

He sounded so sure of himself—so smug! She had an urge to leave him there with his hired lackey and go home on her own. Before she could act on her impulse, he was ushering her into the cab.

"Take us to a nice, quiet bar. No students," Greg told the driver.

"I really should be getting home," Martha said.

"Why interrupt your mother's bridge game? You certainly aren't going to work anymore tonight."

57

"No, but I'm a little tired."

His only response was to lean over, push away her hair, and nuzzle her ear. His breath was warm and ticklish and she giggled, apparently pleasing him because he planted a soft little kiss on her delicate lobe.

"Don't." A negative message came out of her mouth, but the rest of her wasn't paying much attention to it. Spasms of sheer pleasure shot through her, and she clutched at Greg's shoulders like a drowning woman.

"If I get a motel room—" he murmured.

"No!"

The cab lurched around a corner, throwing her up against him as they slid to one side on the slippery old leather seat.

"I should've driven," she muttered just before he gathered her into his arms for a series of kisses that almost made her forget her reservations.

The only thing imaginative about the Dancing Unicorn was its name. Inside, the bar was dark and rather smoky, but it did give an illusion of intimacy. The privacy of the patrons was insured by booths with dividers holding plants between them. Martha slid across a wooden seat, and slipped her navy coat from her shoulders. Across from her Greg laid his overcoat on the seat and leaned across the black-top table to make himself heard over an Irish Rover's tape being piped in loudly enough to fill a football stadium.

"Your cab driver is some tour guide," she shouted.

"I'll take care of it."

He motioned to a young waiter in a lavender T-shirt with the bar's logo, saying something Martha couldn't hear; she did see a bill change hands and disappear into the side pocket of a tight pair of jeans. Moments later the music changed to a softly played ballad. She wasn't used

58

to people who altered their surroundings with the flick of a bill; she wasn't sure it pleased her.

"What would you like?" Greg asked.

"I don't know." She didn't even know if she wanted to be there with him.

"How about an ice cream drink? Brandy Alexander?"

She wasn't too confused to calculate the calories in that concoction.

"No, thank you. I'll have some white wine."

He ordered wine for her and an imported dark beer for himself, sitting back on the seat and saying little but watching her intently. Wanting to say something, she fell back on what she thought was a safe subject.

"I did find a few recipes you may be able to adapt. How does sweet potato soufflé sound?"

"I'll have to think about it when I'm not drunk."

"Drunk?" He'd only had one drink at the party; he couldn't possibly be intoxicated.

"That's the way I feel looking at you. Do you know, you have the most beautiful blue eyes?"

The waiter delivered their drinks along with a napkin-lined basket of popcorn. Martha sipped at her wine to avoid meeting Greg's gaze. He let his beer sit for a minute then took a large swallow.

"It's warm in here." He looked cool and composed.

"Yes, I guess it is."

"Would you like me to hang your coat somewhere?"

"No, no, it's fine." She drank another sip of wine but nothing that came in a glass could calm her tonight, not with Greg so close, watching her so intently.

"I'm sorry about dropping in without calling first. I had a hectic week."

"It's all right. I imagine you're really rushed with

59

plans for the new restaurants." She was desperate to talk about a safe, nonpersonal subject.

"Not too busy to make a phone call," he said sharply.

It took her a moment to realize his anger was directed at himself.

"I didn't want to come back here," he said.

"Then you shouldn't have," she snapped, feeling hurt.

"Do you want to know why I didn't want to come?"

"I'm not sure I do." This was a cowardly lie!

"I'll tell you anyway. You're too attractive, and this is a bad time for me to start any kind of relationship."

"I can understand that you're very busy," she said coolly.

"Not just busy. I'm always that. I need to rethink my future. It's not the right time for me to make any kind of commitment."

"I feel the same way," she said hoarsely, hoping she'd wake up and find this whole evening had been a dream.

"I—I'm . . ."

Hearing him grope for words put her a little more at ease. He didn't finish his thought.

"We can dance if you like," he said, gesturing at a square of polished floor where one couple was swaying somewhat in tune with the soft music which was still playing.

"All right."

If they were dancing, she thought, they wouldn't have to talk. He led the way, taking her in his arms with his hand on her waist. He wasn't doing any recognizable step but his sense of rhythm was marvelous; she floated in his arms, totally at ease with his lead. It seemed the most natural thing in the world when he hugged her closer, cradling her head on his shoulder.

They left their second drinks untouched on the table,

hardly able to believe they'd been in the Dancing Unicorn for nearly two hours. This time they had to walk up the street to find their cab, waking the driver to take them back to Alexandria.

"Wait just a minute," Greg said to her in front of her house, moving to the trunk of the taxi with the driver.

Carrying a nylon travel bag he walked to the gate with her.

"Where are you staying?" she asked, surprised that he'd sent the cab away.

"You told me not to get a motel room."

"A motel room for the two of us was what I meant!" she gasped in astonishment.

"Come on," he said, smiling widely as he urged her along. "I don't think your mother will mind. . . ."

"We don't have a guest room! Did she invite you to stay?"

"No, but all I need is your couch. It looks long enough."

"Surely the Old Town Holiday Inn would have a vacancy."

"I suppose I could try. How far is it?"

"Not far at all. I'll get my car."

"Martha." His voice had a vulnerable, pleading quality she hadn't heard before. "Would it be so terrible if I sacked out on your couch?"

"I suppose not, but . . ." There were hundreds of reasons why he shouldn't, but she couldn't think of one to tell him.

"I promise I won't even think about sneaking past your mother to your room."

"I should hope not!"

He opened the gate for her, motioning her to go ahead into the passageway. She wasn't quite sure how they managed to get squeezed together in the narrow space between the brick walls, but when he kissed her, she didn't care. The age-worn bricks were unyielding behind her back, but his arm cushioned her head. She heard his bag drop to the pavement, then his other hand moved to the side of her throat, caressing the soft skin above her coat collar as his tongue ravaged her mouth, driving her wild with its provocative thrusts.

"You taste wonderful." His voice sounded ragged and she was beyond speech herself. "Is your mother a sound sleeper?"

"No! I wouldn't dream—I couldn't!"

"A motel then?"

"Absolutely not! I hardly know you!" She managed to squeeze beyond him, leaving him to follow if he insisted.

"Do you operate on a time schedule? Date one a chaste kiss, date two a little tongue kissing, date three—"

"You're not funny!" She reached the back door, fumbling for her key and trying to sound unruffled. Panic spilled into her voice and she was so flustered, Greg had to find the key for her.

The bridge game was over; only the overhead light in the kitchen was on, but it seemed harsh and revealing. Martha knew her hair was in a state of disarray, curls spilling in every direction, and her lips felt swollen. She felt dazed but hoped Greg didn't realize how much she wanted to be kissed again.

"I wouldn't say no to a cup of coffee, if you have decaffeinated," he said.

"We do."

It didn't matter what she drank; she'd never be able to sleep with Greg in the house and apparently he planned on staying.

"Where can I get ready for bed—for the couch I

mean?" He was standing under the archway to the living room, his traveling bag slung over his shoulder.

"There's only one bathroom. On the second floor. Mother's probably asleep across the hall. The spare room on that floor used to be my father's office. There's no bed in there."

"I understand."

She went through the procedure of making coffee without thinking about it, not sure what it was he understood.

When he returned, his shirt was hanging loose.

"I want to tell you about my new idea," he said.

"Sit down." She gestured at the table, setting two thick mugs on the painted surface.

"I still want your ideas for the menu." He sat, watching as she poured steaming coffee into the mugs.

"I think we have some cake left from the bridge party," she offered.

"None for me, thanks."

His eyes never left her. She could feel them on her back when she returned the coffee pot to the counter.

"Tell me about your family," she said, sitting across from him, reluctant to hear his new idea because she wasn't sure how helpful her research would be on the menu. She couldn't imagine anything else he might ask her to do—professionally.

"There's just my parents and my younger sister. She's married and lives in Joliet. I want you to be my figure-head."

"Your what?"

"Like the Kentucky Colonel," he said, "only beautiful."

She was stunned into silence.

"You'd represent my colonial restaurants, appear on TV and in other ads, endorse the food, that sort of thing.

It's the best idea I've had in years: the master cook who's also a gorgeous woman."

"I couldn't do something like that!" She was aghast.

"Why not? I saw one of your TV appearances. You're poised and photogenic. You have a reputation in the culinary field. You're a natural for the job. I don't know why I didn't think of it right away."

"But I'm a researcher. I take my work seriously!"

"Do you think I don't?"

"I'd be like the clown who sells hamburgers!"

"Hardly," he said dryly, his tone telling her he'd expected a more enthusiastic response. "The whole idea is to give the restaurants a wholesome image. I thought you could wear a colonial costume."

"This doesn't sound like something I could do."

"Of course you can." He stood up, hovering over her. "It will pay better than writing cookbooks."

Remembering the tiny advance from the Sugar Glen Society, she knew how right he was. Still, she couldn't see herself as a food-chain promoter, flouncing around in a costume for TV commericals. It would ruin her reputation. No one would take her research seriously after that. It would be the same as jumping out of a giant toilet bowl or having bushels of cotton balls dumped on her head. That kind of thing was for actors, not a culinary historian. She'd be horrid at it: stiff and awkward and embarrassed.

"I don't like to see you frowning like that." He bent over and pushed away a tendril of hair, lightly kissing her brow. "Give it some thought. You don't have to say yes tonight."

"I don't see how I can," she said more to herself than to him.

He turned off the coffee maker and the kitchen lights,

moving into the living room by the light of an old brass floor lamp he switched on. Martha followed him, feeling as though her whole life was being turned topsy-turvy.

"Do you still want to see my recipes?" she asked.

"Umm?"

He was sitting on the couch, stretching his legs.

"My recipes!"

"Sure. Put your package together and send it to my office along with your bill. Did I give you my business card?"

She shook her head.

"I'll get one." He went to his suit jacket lying on the back of a rocker and removed a white card from an inner pocket. "Here."

She held it without looking at it, reacting like an adolescent to the light brush of his fingers against hers, wanting to prolong the slightest contact even though the man himself made her more than a little apprehensive. What did he really want from her? He seemed to spring one surprise after another.

It was no surprise when he kissed her again. His lips were warm and his hands gentle on her throat, but he kept space between their bodies. She couldn't believe how badly she wanted to be crushed against him again, but he said a soft "good night" and moved away.

As if his presence in the house wasn't enough to disturb her sleep, now she had to think about his proposal. Could she possibly be a figurehead for his restaurants? Would doing so ruin her career? Would the money be enough compensation for what she'd have to sacrifice: her reputation, possibly even her integrity? Maybe his restaurants would serve terrible food that made a mockery of genuine colonial cookery. Then where would she be?

Where did she want to be? An honest little whisper came from the depths of her mind: she wanted to be in Greg's arms.

The bedside clock showed how futile her attempt to sleep had been. It was past three A.M., and she was all tied up in knots. Giving up, she crept barefoot across the floorboards, slowly descending to the second and then the first floor. She told herself hot chocolate would help but knew the rattle of the pan and the thud of the refrigerator door might wake Greg.

Moving cautiously in the dark room to see if he was deep in slumber, she moved toward the bulky outline of the couch. There Greg was lying quietly on his side, a thick old quilt pulled up to his ear. The couch wasn't quite long enough; he had to keep his knees bent to fit.

Squealing with startled fright, she tried to pull away when a hand darted out and captured a fistful of her fleecy robe.

"Your kitchen faucet drips, did you know?" he asked, not letting go.

"I'm sorry. Is it keeping you awake?"

"No, a little thing like that wouldn't rob me of sleep."

Something apparently had, because her footsteps had been too quiet to wake him; she knew how to avoid every squeaky spot on the old stairs.

"I thought I'd have some hot chocolate," she said awkwardly, trying to tug her way free.

"That might wake me."

"Well, yes, I thought of that."

"You wanted to wake me?"

"No! I decided against the chocolate."

"You've lost me somewhere, darling," he murmured, sitting up but not releasing his hold on her robe.

"Let go of my robe, please." She reached out to yank

66

on it, accidently brushing his bare shoulder with the back of her hand.

"Your couch is too short." He drew her closer, using the robe as a pulley around her legs.

"I was afraid it might be." A bit sarcastically she added, "I'm sorry if you're uncomfortable."

"Sorry enough to invite me upstairs?" he teased.

"Certainly not!"

"Are you going to fix your hot chocolate or kiss me?"

"Neither! I'm going back to bed!"

His throaty chuckle followed her up the stairs.

CHAPTER FOUR

It never occurred to her that Greg would leave before she woke up.

Although it was after nine, she was bleary-eyed from lack of sleep, coming downstairs in her robe after brushing her teeth and dousing her face with cold water. The couch was empty except for the neatly folded patchwork quilt, and there was no sign of Greg or his clothing. Her mother was in the kitchen reading the paper and sipping her coffee.

"We had a visitor last night," Martha said, puzzled but cautious.

"Oh, yes, dear. Greg explained about not getting a motel room."

"Where is he?"

"He had to catch a plane. I offered to wake you to drive him to the airport but he said since the subway goes right past International, he'd just run over and get on it."

"Where was he going?"

"I think he mentioned Omaha."

He was probably going there to buy meat or something. There was no reason to feel so letdown, she told herself. His absence gave her more time to decide whether to accept his offer.

"The faucet is dripping. We'll have to call a plumber tomorrow," Martha said, wondering why he didn't have buyers to run around the country for him. He undoubtedly did; his trip could be purely personal.

"I don't suppose we could do anything ourselves?" her mother asked without much hope.

"I'm afraid it needs a whole new faucet unit."

"We should make a list of all our other little plumbing problems. They don't charge any more if they work for a full hour."

"He could check the bathroom. I'm tired of jiggling the handle."

"We probably need something new there too," Fleury said dejectedly.

"Someday we'll renovate and all the old plumbing will go," Martha promised, feeling even more glum because now there was a way to make it happen.

The prospect of joining the ranks of gravel-voiced hamburger hucksters and orange-haired clowns wasn't any more appealing than it had been the night before. Until she made her decision, it seemed best not to mention it to her mother.

That afternoon Fleury watched Martha make sweetbread pie using one of the Sugar Glen recipes that needed testing. The baked filling was grayish, and neither of them liked it at all. It was the prized recipe of the society's president, so Martha was torn between including a bad-tasting recipe or offending the woman who'd recommended her for the job. Sometimes she hated her work!

She was still cleaning the kitchen when the phone rang.

"Martha, this is Greg. I'm sorry I missed you this morning."

"I didn't know you had to leave so early. I would've fixed breakfast and driven you to the airport."

"I thought you deserved to sleep late."

69

His voice made her feel pampered, and warmth flowed to her cheeks.

"Well, I'm sorry." Why was she apologizing? What she really regretted was not seeing him again.

"From here I go to New York City."

Even the prospect of having him on the East Coast was mildly cheering.

"Then I've decided I need a vacation," he continued.

"Everyone does occasionally."

"I have a room reserved Thursday through Saturday. Your couch is too short."

"I'll see you then?"

"There's no way you can avoid it!"

She wanted to avoid giving an answer to his new offer but even that didn't dull her eagerness to see him again.

"I won't try."

"Thursday then."

"I'll look forward to it," she said softly.

"So will I, so will I."

Monday, Fleury had another long phone conversation with their insurance agent, Mr. Houston. She tried to explain everything he'd said to her daughter, but Martha didn't understand all of it the first time through.

"You do understand what a Peer Review Committee is, don't you?" her mother asked, sounding unusually impatient when her daughter's responses were vague.

"A group of doctors."

"If they decide the Baltimore surgeon charged too much, the insurance company won't pay the full amount. They'll only pay what the committee decides is a fair fee. It's all spelled out in our policy."

"Can't the lawyers you worked for do something?" Martha asked, too worried to eat the rather excellent beans she'd baked all day in the oven built into the fire-place.

"Not until we find out what the Peer Committee decides. If they say the fee's too high, the insurance company won't have to pay the rest of the bill, and I'll have to pay all those thousands of dollars."

"We'll have to," her daughter corrected her, even though this wasn't comforting to Fleury.

"If only I hadn't gone to visit Janice. . . ."

"Old college friends should keep in touch."

"But I still feel responsible. . . ."

"The other driver was drunk, Mother! There was nothing you could do."

"And they can't even find him so we can sue him!"

Feeling helpless when it came to consoling her mother, she changed the subject. "Do you like these beans?"

Fleury took her first bite. "You definitely should include this recipe in your new book."

Martha wasn't sure; nothing was tasting very good to her these days.

Thursday she had her hair cut, pleased with a style that was short on the sides but retained her long, loose curls in back. Twenty dollars for a cut strained the weekly budget, but Fleury raved about the change in her daughter's appearance.

In spite of her troubles, Martha was aware of a glow on her face, an almost feverish anticipation that not even the cloudy surface of her mirror could dull. Greg had called her twice that week without mentioning his job offer. She was meeting him at the airport that evening.

Her black cords were looser than they had been, slenderizing a bottom that tended to look a little plump in slacks. With them she wore a pale blue angora sweater with a little Peter Pan collar. She wanted Greg to see her own clothes, not the more sophisticated ones borrowed from her mother.

She knew the number of Greg's flight, but the list of arrivals showed the plane was running late. Browsing in a gift shop, drinking coffee purchased in a crowded cafeteria line, and checking her appearance in the women's room didn't kill enough time. She bought a magazine and flipped through it, but no article ever written could hold her attention this evening. She wanted to see Greg so badly it scared her. Maybe his only interest was in hiring her; maybe he was charming and seductive with every woman he met. Maybe . . .

Unless there was another delay, his plane was landing. For a few panicky moments she wanted to run away. She was expecting too much from this meeting!

Steeling herself for disappointment, she imagined the bad things that could happen. He might pressure her about representing his restaurants and be angry when she couldn't give him an immediate answer. Worse, he might not be at all interested in her as a person.

Weaving through the airport crowd in a daze, she found a spot against a wall where she could see Greg before he saw her. It was silly to believe his face would tell her all she wanted to learn, but she felt more secure knowing she could still change her mind about meeting him.

At first sight he didn't look at all the way she'd expected. Instead of his tailored overcoat and a suit, he was wearing a short leather coat and faded jeans, swinging a nylon carryall over one shoulder. Watching him walk rapidly in her direction, she was too mesmerized to move. Then, amazingly, she was in his arms, totally oblivious to the parade of passengers streaming past them. His kiss banished her doubts like the sun dissolving a morning fog. She couldn't think of anything but how wonderful it was to be with him again.

"I feel like I've been away five weeks, not five days," he said, hugging her against his side as they walked toward the exit.

Skirting piles of luggage and clusters of travelers, they made their way to the exit then walked to the parking area where her car was waiting.

"I can't quite believe," he said, drawing her against him for a lingering kiss, "how much I've missed you."

"I missed you too."

In her own ears the words sounded inadequate, but her kiss wasn't, taking away his breath and leaving her weak-kneed and shaky.

"Do you want to drive?" she asked, feeling too light-headed to trust herself behind the wheel.

"Sure. Whatever you like." He landed a loud kiss on her chin.

As he drove, they spoke in fragments, anticipating each other's questions, leaving them only partially answered.

"How was your—" he asked.

"Busy, I—"

"With the cookbook?"

"My concentration wasn't—"

"Me too! My concentration wasn't—"

"Crazy, I guess."

"Tell me," he urged.

"What?"

"Missed me?"

"Should I?"

"As much as I missed you?"

"Yes."

He drove in the slow lane, letting traffic pass him,

touching her hand, her knee, her thigh, fleeting caresses eloquent in their restraint.

"Better pay attention," he said, meaning himself.

"Yes, heavy traffic."

"Free till Sunday."

"No work?"

"Only pleasure."

"No flying off?" She wanted to be darn sure of that.

"No, I'm grounded right here."

Her heart was singing; he hadn't come just to press her about his offer. This beautiful, wonderful man did want to be with her.

Her mother was so obvious, Martha would've been embarrassed any other time. Tonight she was grateful when Fleury went upstairs hours before her usual late bedtime.

"I hope I'll see you again, Greg," she said, moving into the hallway thumping her walking cane.

"You can count on it," he said heartily.

"Do you have to check into your hotel?" Martha asked, so unused to being coy she didn't recognize it in herself.

"No, I have a guaranteed reservation."

"Are you hungry?"

"No, it was a dinner flight."

"Something to drink?" She tried to remember if they had anything besides cooking sherry.

He stood, shaking his head, walking over to the couch where she was sitting on the edge at one end.

"There was something I meant to ask you," he said, looking down on her, his eyes reminding her of deep, dark, unfathomable wells.

"Greg—"

"No, don't say anything, not yet."

74

He sat beside her and scooped her into his arms, locking his mouth over hers with unhurried relish.

"I've imagined that—and more—a thousand times this week."

His sweater was cashmere, downy-soft under her fingers, the V neck showing dark hairs sprinkled thickly over his chest. Too enthralled to worry about whether she was being aggressive, she slid her hands under the back of it, delighting in the smooth, warm skin of his back.

"Oh, baby . . ." he murmured.

His tongue filled her mouth, sending hot sensations through her entire body.

"I like your hair," he said softly, holding her against him, stroking the soft angora that covered her shoulders and back.

"Thank you."

She reached up and separated one of the silver hairs that gave a sheen to the black strands around it. It was more beautiful than the precious metal, and she was sure he'd only be more attractive as his hair turned white.

"I think I have too many gray hairs to pluck them out," he teased.

"Never do that! I love salt and pepper hair."

"Surely I'm not that gray!"

"Not yet, but your hair will be beautiful that way."

"That's a new thought." He held her close, taking deep breaths, curling a lock of hair around his finger.

Sitting close beside him in the crook of his arm, her face against the softness of his sweater, she felt a marvelous contentment seep through her.

"Tell me all about your week," he said.

The attraction between them was so powerful, she felt warmly grateful to him for not pushing her into an impossible situation. She couldn't make love in the house with her mother upstairs but her will to refuse him had crumbled.

"It was uneventful. I mailed you some recipes. Did you get them?"

"Not yet. I worked in my office this morning."

"I suppose they'll arrive tomorrow or Saturday."

"Most likely." He held her hand in his, palm up, tracing the lines with one long finger.

"Are you reading my palm?"

"No, I'm not interested in predictions. I make my own future."

"Sometimes fate intervenes."

"Maybe. Luck can present opportunities, but it's up to people to do something with them." He closed her fingers over her palm, covering them with his. "What are you going to do with your opportunity?"

She knew exactly what he meant. "Will I run with the ball or fumble?"

"Something like that."

"It's not quite that simple. I have other commitments —a whole career of my own." She knew this didn't sound very convincing to him.

"I'm offering to make you rich and famous." His grin took the hardness out of his words. "Your face is just what I want."

He touched her cheek and she wasn't at all sure he was talking about restaurant promotions. What could possibly be wrong with any job that let her be near him? When his lips covered hers, she sensed there was an unspoken agreement between them. It was so easy to forget everything but the sweetness of his kiss.

"Tomorrow I want you to show me the town." He stood, pulling her up and holding her against him.

"Are you leaving already?"

76

"Do you want to come with me?"

She did but couldn't say so.

"That couch isn't big enough for anything I have in mind," he said with a soft laugh. "Come to my room."

"I don't think so." She knew this wasn't a brilliant answer.

"It's okay." He lightly kissed her forehead. "I don't want to rush you into anything."

Did that include her decision on whether to work for him? She was afraid he'd insist on an answer while he was in Alexandria.

He refused her offer to drive him to his hotel.

"It's not that far. I need a good walk to get the kinks out." He kissed her lightly and left, but not before she read the reluctance in his eyes. Could she hope that he regretted even a brief separation as much as she did?

At that moment she would've said yes to anything he asked. Only later, alone in her room, did her doubts return. Did she really want her life turned upside down so she could promote a restaurant chain? How much would she have to travel? Was her mother well enough to be left alone for long periods? Did she want to give up her culinary research and writing?

Away from Greg's compelling presence, she wasn't nearly as happy as she wanted to be. Why did her reluctance diminish when he was with her, only to return more forcefully as soon as he left? Was he steering her into something she'd regret for a long, long time?

Entertaining Greg was a sheer pleasure. He was so excited about Old Town Alexandria, he made her see it with fresh eyes. They toured the Carlyle Mansion, where the blue paper wrapped around breakables shipped to the colony had once been used to dye paint for the walls, then visited the apothecary shop where Martha Washington ordered castor oil and George picked up his mail.

For lunch they went to Gadsby's Tavern, and Martha told him how a young naval officer, John Paul Jones, had helped a Frenchman order dinner and lodging there when no one could understand him.

"Let me guess," Greg said. "It must have been Lafayette."

"On his way to join the Continental Army!"

His enthusiasm pleased her immensely; in fact, his companionship was so enjoyable, she wanted to share everything she knew with him. It took a little restraint not to sound like a history professor!

Like most of the items on Gadsby's menu, the clams could've been served in the eighteenth century. They were delicious, but it was inevitable that they reminded Greg of his own restaurant plans.

"You're keeping me in terrible suspense, you know," he said as they lingered over coffee.

"Am I?" This time she knew she was being coy. "I've always wanted to write a thriller."

"It's thrilling for me to be with you, but I'm not talking about books right now."

"Do you like to read?" Such obvious evasiveness pricked her conscience.

"When I have time, which isn't very often. I want you to know, I was only half-committed to starting a new chain before I met you. I needed the challenge but there wasn't the excitement or risk that went with building up the Turkey Havens."

"You're having second thoughts about the colonial restaurants?" she asked hopefully.

"None at all now! I love the idea of serving old-fashioned wholesome food at reasonable prices. With your help I can sell the public on eating it."

"I don't think I can be that helpful." She had visions of the décolletage in a colonial era costume, with her breasts pushed up like two ripe honeydew melons and her waist sucked in by a corset.

"To me, even a pot of beans would taste delicious if I imagined you cooking it. My customers will feel the same way."

"Do you use an advertising agency? Maybe they'll have other ideas."

"I have other ideas too," he said, leaning across the table to rest his hand on hers, "but they all have something to do with you."

"If we're going to see Mount Vernon today . . ."

She never tired of the first president's home; the wonderful old kitchen with bundles of herbs hanging to dry had inspired her interest in colonial cooking before she took her first home economics class in high school. On the way back they stopped at Christ Church and stood beside the enclosed pew of the Washington family. With Greg beside her, she wasn't imagining a white-wigged congregation in the graceful old church. The scene that popped into her mind had more to do with orange blossoms and bridal veils.

Angry at herself for letting her imagination run wild, she practically ran from the hushed dignity of the church. Greg wanted her to work for him, not share his life!

Sensing her mood change, he drove back to Old Town without saying much and parked near the inn where he was staying.

"Where would you like to have dinner?" he asked.

"I could fix something at home."

Her mother was going to Lydia's for dinner and bridge, an exciting invitation because it meant Fleury was well enough to begin resuming some of her normal activities. Martha didn't have to drive her mother there; another friend was picking her up.

"I'd take you out tonight," he insisted.

"All right, but I should change first," she said.

"I will too. Come up and wait for me."

Going to his room didn't seem like a very good idea, but she had a totally irrational urge not to let him out of her sight. She used to hate fairy tales where the princes kept going off on mysterious missions and not returning. Greg would fly off to his own world all too soon, and until he did she wanted to be with him as much as possible.

They were alone in the elevator that took them to the sixth floor of the hotel, which made her wonder what it would be like to be stuck between floors with Greg. She always sized up fellow passengers in case the elevator broke down, trying to decide whether she'd chance their company or try escaping through the hatch in the roof. With Greg she'd definitely wait to be rescued.

The room had two queen-size beds, dark sandalwood carpeting, and a view of brick-paved walks and the street below. Martha sat down on one of the upholstered chairs by the window and seized the nearest piece of reading material in an attempt to appear nonchalant. It was the room-service menu.

"Anything look good?" Greg asked as he hung his leather coat beside a dark gray suit.

"Oh! No, I don't think so."

Now he thought she wanted to eat in his room!

"Let me see." He perched on the arm of her chair, balancing on one leg, letting the other hang so close to her arm she could almost feel the heat of his body. "There're plenty of choices: steak, chicken, seafood, lamb, veal."

"Where were you thinking of going for dinner?" she asked.

"I was going to let you suggest a place."

The only one that came to mind in this tight situation was the dining room at the Smithsonian, and she probably couldn't find her membership card. Lining up for food wasn't at all what Greg had in mind anyway! Why wasn't her brain working?

He leaned closer, brushing her cheek with a kiss. "I wanted to do that by Washington's pew but I wasn't sure George's ghost would approve. Maybe he would approve of what I wanted to do in his bedroom. I don't think the old general was as stuffy as his pictures make him look."

"His false teeth bothered him." She was feeling hot and bothered herself. Being alone in a bedroom with Greg seemed more unreal than plantation life at Mount Vernon.

"I've tried to be a model of gentlemanly behavior," he said teasingly, reaching out and caressing the back of her neck with both hands.

"You mean you've been on good behavior?"

"I certainly have tried, ma'am."

"Are you still trying?"

"You tell me."

The touch of his lips on hers was such a blessed relief to the yearning she'd felt all day that nothing else mattered. When he stood and drew her into his arms, not a trace of unwillingness clouded her mind. She was exactly where she wanted to be.

"You are very special," Greg said slowly, pronouncing each word as though making a momentous discovery.

81

Her blazer had seen better days. When it fell to the floor, she thought good riddance. Her blouse was the next piece of clothing Greg helped her shed.

His hands were cold, making her shiver as he unfastened the catch on her bra, but they warmed as he circled her ribs, sliding below her breasts to tenderly cup them. While his thumbs kneaded the rosy tips, his mouth roamed over her face and throat, stoking her desire until she felt hot and tingly all over. Slowly she inched her fingers up under his sweater, appreciating its softness and its whiteness, which made his skin look tan and his eyes almost black. After she helped him slip out of the sweater, he leaned down and kissed each of her shoulders, running his tongue over the smooth slopes.

He covered her breasts with the palms of his hands and squeezed gently, opening and closing his mouth over hers at the same time. She, in turn, reached out, luxuriating in the thick matting of hair on his chest.

"I want to see all of you," he murmured, unsnapping her jeans.

"The windows . . ."

The late afternoon sun held a promise of spring, but the street was shadowy. A sudden shyness made her imagine that hundreds of people were looking up at this room.

"I'll pull the curtains," he said.

The comforting dimness lasted only a moment; Greg turned on the lamp hanging over the chairs. She felt branded by her defects: little skin flaws on her back, the extra bit of padding here and there, the sharpness of her shoulder blades, the scars on her knees from trying to roller skate on brick sidewalks. Then he returned to her, kissing her mouth, her throat, her breasts, peeling away her remaining garments with a hushed reverence that made her melt in his arms.

"You're so beautiful," he whispered, just holding her against him.

He stepped out of his jeans and shorts with a total lack of self-consciousness that made the last of hers vanish. Ordinary people weren't supposed to feel this way; what was happening between them belonged in the realm of fantasy. He was everything to her at that moment, and the rest of the world seemed to fade away.

His shoulders and forearms were hard, his hips narrow with tight, round buttocks and muscular, hairy thighs. She was dazed by the magnificence of his body, which her hands boldly explored, and while she did so his kisses roved over her. There was no haste in his gentle caresses. He seemed to take pleasure in every part of her from the tip of her little finger to her slender ankles.

"My golden girl," he murmured.

Turning away for an instant, he pulled back the bedspread and covers so abruptly that she was momentarily startled. Taking a small half-step backward, she remembered her conviction that a friendship should ripen slowly. With Greg things were going so fast she felt disoriented. Like a carnival-goer who wants off in the middle of a roller-coaster ride, she knew the conclusion was inevitable, but that didn't stop her from feeling a little frightened. A moment later when he opened his arms and she came to him, basking in his slow, sweet kisses, she forgot her fears.

"You're beautiful," he murmured.

This man who was brusque and decisive about everything else was suddenly tenderly hesitant, kissing her face and neck, making these moments of time seem precious with his unhurried joy in their closeness. Sitting on the edge of the bed, he took her hand and separated her fingers, kissing the spaces between them until she circled his neck with her arms and flung herself against him.

She loved their playful tussling. He didn't ask questions. He didn't ask her what she did or didn't like. He knew. Clinging to his shoulders, meeting his thrusts, she surrendered to joy, exulting in the culmination of their lovemaking.

While he dozed, she lay with her cheek against his arm. If she was superstitious about anything, it was the strange workings of fate. The good and the bad had to balance; she couldn't be this happy now without paying later. What was the worst that could happen? He'd taken precautions so she wouldn't get pregnant. He'd promised nothing, so she shouldn't be disappointed if this time with Greg was only a brief interlude in her life.

The very worst thing would be for him to leave her. Just thinking about it made her stir restlessly beside him.

"Are you okay?" he murmured sleepily.

"Just cold," she lied, moving down to the end of the bed to find the top sheet and blanket, pulling both over the two of them.

"I didn't lure you here," he said, coming awake and leaning on one elbow to see her face in the well-lit room. "I had good intentions about changing and going to dinner."

"I believe you." She smiled up at him, inviting the kiss that he bestowed on the tip of her nose. "Don't kiss me there!"

"Is that the only place that's out of bounds?"

"I'll have to think about that."

"Think fast, because we're going to take a nice warm shower, then order one of everything from room service."

"You're that hungry?"

"No, I want to keep you here that long."

Later she wouldn't remember what they ate for dinner, but she'd never forget their shower, soaping each other with handfuls of bubbly suds, rubbing slippery bodies together while needlelike spray cascaded over them, making love with her back against cold wall tiles and her legs wrapped around his steely thighs and hips, trusting him totally and not being disappointed.

"Spend the night here," he urged later that evening.

"My mother will worry."

"Call her."

"And ask permission for an overnight?"

They both grinned.

"Why do you live at home?" he asked.

"I lived away for a couple of years."

"Why did you move back?"

She didn't want to talk about her relationship with Peter going on the skids. "Finances for one thing. My mother was having a hard time hanging on to the house. Apartment rents here are high. It made sense to share expenses."

"And look after each other?"

"A little of that, too, I suppose."

"Would your mother mind so much if you didn't come home tonight?"

"Maybe not, but she'd *know.*"

He laughed, then kissed her soundly. "I know about mothers. Mine would start making a guest list."

She wanted to ask why he'd never married. Being too busy seemed like an inadequate reason. "You have that kind of mother too?"

"She's very frustrated with me."

"Aren't you a nice son?"

"I don't think my main mission in life is to produce

grandbabies for her to spoil. If you have to go home, I'll drive you and walk back."

"You can bring my car here for the night."

"I like to walk at night."

"Do you do that in Chicago?"

"Sometimes. I can take care of myself."

She didn't doubt that.

At home she reached her third-floor room before he turned the corner and walked out of sight. From her window she saw him walking with his head down, seemingly studying the bricks underfoot. Did he regret making love? she wondered. Did he feel an obligation that was unpleasant to him? She tried to remember every moment they'd spent together. Some of the little things he'd said puzzled her. Was he worried she'd turn down his offer to represent his restaurants if he didn't continue their affair?

Her fears were exactly the opposite. She didn't know how to reject his job offer without losing him.

CHAPTER FIVE

The living room was chilly, and Martha hugged herself for warmth, heading for the kitchen and a hot cup of coffee. Her blue quilted slippers padded across the old rug. Its floral pattern was worn away in spots and she and her mother had talked of cutting out the better sections and using them as throw rugs, but the varnished floorboards underneath were warped and worn.

Fleury was sleeping late, so Martha economized by not turning up the thermostat, relying on the coffee to warm her. The kitchen seemed even colder, so she carried her cup to the living room, wrapped a granny-square afghan made by her Aunt Maxine around her shoulders, and turned on the TV. The programming hadn't changed since she was a kid; Saturday morning was still cartoon time. The animated characters on two channels were strangers to her, but a third was featuring an old friend, Bugs Bunny. She laughed lightheartedly as she watched the lively antics of Elmer Fudd and his wisecracking tormentor. But her laughter stopped abruptly when she remembered what had happened with Greg the night before. She wished she could think only about the tenderness they'd shared and the pleasure they'd given each other, without feeling the pressure of deciding one way or the other about his business offer.

Why was adult life so complicated? Actually, being a

kid was no snap either. She remembered her first major crush in the third grade. He was the son of an army colonel working at the Pentagon; she worshipped him from afar, even forgiving him when he brought a garter snake to school and chased other girls with it. One day he gave her one of his Twinkies at lunch time. His hands were dirty when he unwrapped it but she ate it anyway, because she loved him. The next week she stayed home with a cold; when she went back to school, he'd disappeared from her life. After several anxious days she worked up enough nerve to ask another boy if her beloved was sick. His father had been transferred.

Emerging from her nostalgic musings, she watched a farmer in overalls extol the virtues of corn cereal. He was a stereotype of a hick, talking as though his mouth were full of mush while he waved a pitchfork. He might sell cereal to kids but his painted-on freckles and straw hair made a mockery of farmers. The actor doing the commercial probably didn't care, she thought, but she certainly wouldn't want to be a caricature of herself, sacrificing her hard-earned reputation to do some silly skit an ad writer had dreamed up. What if the food in Greg's restaurants was just ordinary run-of-the-mill fare? How could she endorse a menu as authentic colonial cookery if none of the chefs mastered the art of preparing it? Chefs! He'd probably hire short-order cooks. He was talking about a chain of franchises, a big business operation, not a fine restaurant like Gadsby's Tavern.

"Goodness, what are you watching?"

Martha was so absorbed in her dilemma, she didn't hear the thud of Fleury's cane.

"I'm really not watching," she fibbed. "The house just seemed to quiet. Did you have fun last night?" The best defense was a good offense.

"It seemed nice to get out of the house."

"You should be able to do it more often now."

"I plan to. Now tell me, how was your evening? I didn't hear you come in."

"You must've been tired. I wasn't that late."

"Did you have fun?"

Greg had given a new definition to the word *fun*, but she couldn't think of anything to tell her mother.

"Yes."

"Just yes? What did you do?"

"Played tourist mostly. Ate at Gadsby's." She didn't mention which meal.

"He'll be here another day?"

"That was his plan." She was torn between a maniacal desire to see him again and sheer dread of discussing his offer.

The phone rang, and she reached it on the second ring, waiting two more to pick it up.

"Martha, you sneak! I'll never forgive you."

Rhonda knew Greg was in town. She wanted the four of them to have dinner at a marvelous seafood place John's dentist had recommended.

"I'm not sure whether—" Martha started to protest.

"Dress up," Rhonda urged. "I found some gorgeous red crepe evening pants at an estate sale. They're embroidered with little gold butterflies, very oriental, and there's yards of material in the legs. This will give me a good excuse to buy a top to go with them."

"You never need an excuse."

Martha's first reaction was negative; she wanted to be alone with Greg. But with a foursome, he wouldn't have a chance to pressure her about his business proposition. Mustering all the enthusiasm possible, she told Rhonda she'd look forward to dinner.

Greg called at noon.

"Good morning, darling. I just took a shower. Can I come over when I'm dressed?"

It wasn't fair to conjure up visions like that over the phone. His bedroom voice purred in her ear, making her visualize his long, lean body. She could almost see the dark whorls of hair sticking to damp skin from his throat to his ankles. Her face flushed, and she put a lid on her almost-total recall of his anatomy.

"Darling?"

"Yes, of course!" she said hastily to make up for her temporary loss of speech.

"We have a lot to talk about." His intimate tone rippled through her like breeze going through a wheat field, disturbing everything without changing a thing.

"I'll walk over," he added. "It looks like a beautiful day."

He exaggerated: the sun was trying to emerge from a fragmented cloud cover, but rain was predicted for later in the day, the cold, penetrating precipitation of late winter.

Fleury expressed a worry that she might be getting a virus; she retired to her room to read in bed, not fooling her daughter for a moment. She was providing a courting parlor. Next she'd want her daughter to bundle in true colonial fashion: two would-be lovers fully dressed in bed with a board between them.

"Good morning." He stepped through the front door and swept her into his arms, giving her a loud, juicy kiss which brought laughter welling up in her throat. "I practiced that one on the back of my hand."

"You didn't!"

"All the way over here."

"You're an incorrigible tease."

"No, until I met you, I was losing my sense of humor. My mother said I was getting as crusty as Uncle Frank."

"Who's Uncle Frank?"

"My grandfather's half-brother. He ran a junkyard on the South Side. In forty years he never left the place except to have his teeth pulled."

"You're making that up!"

"No, there's a kernel of truth in everything I say."

"That little?" She led the way to the living room. "Where's your mother?"

"Upstairs in bed. She's decided to have a virus."

"I'll run up and say hello."

Martha encouraged him: she was willing to bet her cookbook advance Fleury was wearing her best peach satin robe.

The laughter from the second floor carried down the stairs. Greg had found someone who appreciated his humor. Martha gave herself a mental kick in the pants for begrudging her mother the pleasure of his company. After they discussed his job offer, she'd probably be the one who was deprived of it.

She started a fresh pot of coffee in the kitchen, then busied herself slicing cranberry bread, one of her week's test recipes. She heard Greg enter the kitchen but didn't turn around.

"Your mother is recovering nicely."

He stood directly behind her, touching the back of her knee with his, snuggling against her, letting his hands roam over the front of her blue-gray sweater. The rough texture of the part-wool yarn felt prickly when he rubbed it against her skin, and she squirmed, dropping her slicing knife.

"It's dangerous to fool with a serrated blade," she warned, tensing when he ran his hands over her bottom.

"I'll have to take my chances. I woke up wanting you. Why did I let you go home?"

"Let me?" She wiggled around to face him, parting her lips when his touched them.

When they surfaced, he reached around her to snatch a bite-sized piece of the berry-filled sweetbread. "Delicious," he said smacking his lips.

"You haven't even tasted it yet."

"I was talking about you, darling."

He slowly chewed the morsel, keeping his eyes on hers.

"Rhonda called about going to dinner."

"I phoned John about something else. He was mad because I didn't stay with them, so I suggested going out tonight."

"I like John."

"So do I. That's why I said we'd go out with them."

"Greg," she asked hesitantly, "don't you think you should've asked me first?"

"If you don't want to, of course we won't."

"I don't mind. It's only . . ."

"You're right, I should've asked you first." He kissed her with so much gusto she forgot about it.

"You'll have to get used to my snappy decisions," he said seriously, tracing the shape of her lips with one finger, parting them so she could nibble the tip. "When we're working together—"

"I'm not sure we will be."

"I'm having my lawyers draw up a contract. We can't go over the details until it's finished, but—"

"Greg, listen. I'm not sure about the promotional part, about being your figurehead."

"I'm thinking of naming them Martha's Inns."

"You can't do that!" Freeing herself, she retreated to

92

the far side of the kitchen table, facing him with consternation on her face.

"The association is great. Martha—Martha Washington, Martha Graves. An inn suggests a warm, homey place."

"The Martha Graves part is all wrong. I'm not at all sure I can do what you want."

He frowned, and there was more determination than compassion in his eyes.

"I know we haven't talked specifics yet but do you have any idea how much money you'd be turning down?"

He looked around the room instead of at her, observing the things that testified to her straitened circumstances: a gas stove her grandmother had used, dingy tan and green linoleum with worn spots showing the black backing, a lace tablecloth mended so many times the design was cockeyed. Her mother had used her very meager resources to help Martha finish college, and the two of them had never caught up.

He was making her feel guilty and she didn't like it. Maybe in his life money made all the difference, but she'd been raised to believe in dignity and pride.

"It's not a matter of money," she said coldly.

"I haven't found many things that aren't."

"Not everyone lives to make money!"

"Is that what you think of me?"

It wasn't, but she didn't know how to say what she was feeling.

"You're assuming that I'll do what you want because you can afford to pay well."

"Are you saying I've offended your blue-blood sensibilities?"

His eyes narrowed, regarding her with undiluted scorn.

Much of the color left his face, and the jagged little scar on his chin stood out more vividly.

Being the target of unrestrained anger was a novel experience for Martha. Fleury rarely went beyond a mild rebuke; her father, when he was most annoyed, had only sent her to her room. She was used to people who calmly reasoned with her, not a man who looked furious enough to throttle her.

"That's an awful thing to say!" She instinctively defended herself but was too shaken to explain how she really felt. "I don't know anything about your restaurants. Maybe I won't even like what you serve."

"I see."

The hardness in his voice was more than she could handle. Hot tears clouded her vision, and she dashed into the living room.

He caught her in a half-tackle that sent them both tumbling onto the couch. His leg pinned both of hers and he held her hands together with one strong hand.

"What are we doing?" he asked calmly.

His anger had passed as quickly as it had flared up, but he looked miserable and drained. Releasing her hands, he studied her face with a wounded expression that bothered her more than his temper.

She shook her head, too upset to talk.

"I'm sorry. I didn't realize myself how much I'd counted on you," he said.

"What you said isn't true. I'm not being snobbish."

His face was expressionless but she could see the doubt in his eyes. Her cheeks were wet with tears but the need to cry passed. She was too unhappy to wash her troubles away that easily.

"You probably have a good reason for not being interested." He moved his leg to release hers. "I'd like to hear it."

"It's just not my thing." She knew how inadequate this sounded.

"Your thing?"

Bad choice of words, she realized, wanting to be held and comforted, not interrogated and doubted. Working for Greg would never work. What she needed from him had nothing to do with a job.

"I'm a researcher," she said, feeling even more inadequate.

"Let's let it rest for now," he said, sounding dejected. "John's picking me up at seven. We'll be here a few minutes later. We can talk after dinner."

They were still going to dinner together. She was so surprised, she didn't protest.

"I'm going now." He stood and went for his coat, buttoning it as she watched in silence.

"I need time to cool off," he said, then left.

Now she knew Gregory Kent had a quick temper and a sharp tongue. Did she deserve to be on the receiving end of both because she didn't want his job?

She went to her room without looking in on Fleury. Dinner with Greg seemed like a pointless ordeal, but she lacked the courage to cancel it. Her instincts told her that he wouldn't drop the issue between them without a much fiercer fight. She didn't feel at all up to it.

Rhonda's sleeveless top reminded Martha of goldfish scales, but the relaxed, good-natured companionship of the Van Looses was just what she needed that evening. Greg was nonchalantly sociable with them, but when his gaze rested on her, the intensity of it made her squirm mentally.

John's dentist may've been right about the food served

at the seafood restaurant, but Martha was too tense to appreciate it. Her baked sole was a bit dry. John and Rhonda raved about their seafood platters with lobster tails, scallops, shrimp, and frog legs. Greg ate his trout almondine with mechanical indifference, not commenting on it.

The rain came, great black sheets of it that soaked Rhonda's fur coat and made her squeal with indignation.

"I told you to wear a raincoat," John said mildly. "Guess we'd better call it an evening. Why don't you drop me and Rhonda off and use my car to take Martha home," he suggested to Greg. "Keep the car as long as you like. I won't need it tomorrow."

"All right, thanks."

Martha's feet were soaked and she wanted to go home —alone. When John and Rhonda left them, she was afraid Greg had no intention of taking her there, not until he persuaded her to accept his "opportunity."

"We'll go back to my room and talk, okay?"

"Not okay! I'd really like to go home," she insisted.

"I'm leaving tomorrow morning. We need to get this cleared up."

"Everything is clear to me."

"It sure as hell isn't clear to me!" He stopped the car by the curb, killing the motor although they weren't close to her house. "You're not going to tell me you can make more money with cookbooks! If I knew what your objections were—"

"You'd try to argue against them until I change my mind."

"Probably," he admitted, a trace of better humor in his voice. "You're not being fair, you know, sending off a lot of negative signals without giving me any reasons I can buy."

Maybe he was right. He didn't know her well enough to guess her thoughts.

"I take my work very seriously," she said slowly.

"I admire you for that."

"There's a lot more to my field than just food. I have to know how people lived and worked, how they divided the labor, why they used the things they did."

"A lot of history, you mean."

"Yes, that's the part I really enjoy, the history."

"What I'm asking you to do won't take all your time. You'll still be able to work on your books."

"Who will trust me with precious old family recipes after they see me on TV selling fast food?"

"Junk food, you mean?" he asked angrily.

"You can't possibly serve the kind of food Gadsby's Tavern does, not in a reasonably priced family restaurant."

"Aren't you being a little too quick, condemning my food before the restaurants even open?"

"I'm not saying you serve bad food!"

"Aren't you? That's the message I'm getting. My lousy food will besmirch your reputation."

"I didn't mean it like that!"

"Of course you did! And it's just the kind of muddleheaded nonsense I should've expected!"

"Just because my brain doesn't work like a cash register—"

"I'm not sure how it works! If you had one grain of business sense, you'd see what Martha's Inns could mean to you!"

"I don't need them!"

"Not if you want to live in genteel poverty! That old house is crumbling around your—"

"That's none of your business!"

"And your mother's accident—"

"That either! Are you going to drive me home or do I walk?"

"Give me one good reason why you shouldn't take my job, and I'll drive you home."

"I don't want to! That's all the reason I need."

"Martha, that's a childish excuse. I think you're afraid of the big world outside your door."

"That's ridiculous!"

"Is it? Why work for peanuts doing little pamphlets? Why not try something that will interest a major publishing house?"

"My work is very specialized!"

"Meaning not many people are interested in it?"

"No! I mean yes, lots of people are."

"I sell more meals in a day than you sell cookbooks in a year, maybe five or ten years."

"That makes everything you want okay? If I'm such a failure, why don't you take back your offer?"

"Because I think it's right for you!"

"You don't know me that well!"

"I know you better than you think!" Roughly embracing her, he ground his mouth against hers.

She didn't want him! She wouldn't kiss him!

"I wish—"

He didn't finish his wish but the misery in his voice did what force couldn't. She returned his kiss, fervently wishing there was nothing between them but love.

"It's not because of yesterday?" he asked. "You're not upset because—"

"No! Oh, no!" Making love made it harder to refuse him, but she didn't want him to misunderstand the way she felt about it. "I wanted to be with you."

There was relief in his sigh. He kissed her more gently,

making a valiant effort to overcome the obstacles presented by separate car seats and a floor shift. The best he managed was a cheek-to-cheek hug.

"We'll put the job on hold for now, darling. Come back to my room with me."

She desperately wanted to, but not until he understood that she wasn't going to take his job, not now, not ever.

His fingers slid under her hair, caressing the back of her neck. It took so little to make her hunger for him: an intimate touch, the lingering brush of his lips, the warmth of his breath on her throat. Ignoring Rhonda's suggestion, she'd worn a simply-cut navy wool suit with her best white silk blouse. Unbuttoning her practical tan raincoat, he fondled her breasts, sliding his hands under the slippery material and coaxing her nipples to throbbing hardness. Steamy moisture fogged the windows, giving an illusion that they were totally isolated in the car, but she pushed his hands away.

"Not here." Her protest sounded weak.

"My room then." He reached for the key still in the ignition.

"Being with you . . ." She groped for words, feeling as though their relationship was balanced on a tightrope at the point of no return. "It has to be separate."

He understood. "I don't like mixing business and pleasure either," he said thoughtfully. "I don't know why it happened with us, but I can't regret it."

"Greg, before we go anywhere, you have to understand."

"Can't we talk later?"

She shook her head. "I'm not going to take your job."

"The only sensible thing to do is read the contract first. You don't know what you're refusing."

"I do know."

"What about your mother? Does she know you're turning me down?"

"She doesn't know anything about it."

"You see, if you were so sure of yourself, you wouldn't be so secretive." He didn't try to hide his anger.

"I just can't do it!"

"You don't want to! You've got some crazy idea that it will tarnish your credentials."

"What you want me to do will change my whole life. I'm not ready for that."

"Will you ever be?" He started the motor, turned on the wipers and defrosters, then impatiently wiped the foggy window with his hand, smearing it without restoring clear visibility.

"Do you always get mad when you don't get your own way?" she asked, knowing they weren't going to his room; they weren't going anywhere together.

"Mad doesn't cover it! I don't know how you can turn down the opportunity of a lifetime for some vague, snooty reason."

"You think money and opportunity are the same thing. Other things matter too!"

He started driving, his silence more wounding than his accusations. Stopping in front of her house, he sat in frozen silence while she hurried out of the car, then drove away as soon as she opened the iron gate.

Forgetting that the paving was wet, she ran across the courtyard, falling on one knee on the slippery flagstone, opening the door as though the hounds of hell were chasing her.

"Martha!" Fleury stood as quickly as possible, startled by her daughter's streak through the house. "Are you all right?"

"I fell. In the courtyard. I'll be fine." She escaped up the stairs without taking off her soggy coat.

He had absolutely no reason to be so terrible to her! People refused jobs all the time. What was right for one person could be totally wrong for another. Any fair-minded person would realize that, even if he owned a thousand restaurants.

The trouble with Gregory Kent was that everything had to be done his way. He wanted to sweep her into his orbit, make her one more satellite revolving around his glittering success. Well, she thought, she was a woman who wasn't for sale. She liked her life, pokey and unproductive as he seemed to think it was. And what right did he have to judge it?

Hours later, when her rage dissipated and disappointment settled on her like fog over the river, she felt an almost overwhelming sense of loss. She'd never regret refusing Greg's job, but she'd always regret losing this chance at love.

CHAPTER SIX

"I brewed a pot of spearmint tea," Fleury said, standing hesitantly in the doorway of Martha's room, "and there's some chicken salad, your favorite, with grapes and walnuts."

"Thanks, but I wasn't going to stop for lunch."

"Or dinner either?" her mother asked critically. "Dear, those recipes have been around for hundreds of years. You don't have to finish the book in a few weeks."

"The sooner, the better," she said grimly, "then I can go on to something more profitable."

"Not if you collapse from malnutrition!"

When her mother used that tone of voice, it was easier to comply than waste time arguing. Martha stood reluctantly, stretching to get a kink out of her back. She wasn't used to typing for hours on end, day after day, but if she kept it up, the book would be done long before the deadline.

"I'll have just a bite," she said absentmindedly to her mother. "You shouldn't have come all the way up here."

"I'm doing just fine. I'll be throwing this wretched cane away any day."

"Better return it to the rental service instead," Martha said, only half teasing.

She was becoming almost as obsessed with saving money as she was with the cookbook. Genteel poverty indeed! Just because they were temporarily short of cash didn't mean she had to sell her soul to the devil! The Lucifer she conjured up in her imagination bore a startling resemblence to Gregory Kent.

Her mother's luncheon was delicious, but Martha suspected it was prompted as much by curiosity as solicitude. Her mother didn't have enough to keep her mind occupied. She was sure Martha was hiding something from her; it bothered her that Greg had disappeared from the scene three weeks ago without a word of explanation from her daughter.

Nibbling at her chicken salad while Martha ate with more haste than enjoyment, Fleury tried again. "The days are getting warmer. I always love to have visitors see Alexandria in the spring. When do you suppose your friend will be coming back?"

"What friend?" Darned if she'd make it easy!

"That young man—the one who started the chain of restaurants."

"He's a friend of Rhonda's and John's. You'd have to ask them."

"I thought the two of you were getting acquainted."

Martha shrugged her shoulders, feigning indifference. "What are you going to wear tonight?"

Her mother was going to a party, escorted by a recently divorced partner in the law firm where she'd worked.

"Oh, I don't suppose it really matters. Carl probably wants to talk about when I can return to work. What do you think of my black dress with the jacket?"

"You've lost too much weight. Wear something pastel." She knew what her mother intended to wear. "The pink. Not many women your age look good in that shade."

103

"I believe you're right! Now if I could only leave this ugly cane at home."

"Don't," Martha said, feeling older than her mother and deeply weary. "Call me before you leave so I can see how you look."

The cookbook was the one thing in her life that was going well; she returned to it as soon as her mother was satisfied she wouldn't starve to death. Stopping to change the ribbon in her typewriter, she stretched, tired from the long day of typing. Tonight she'd proofread the latest copy and—

The third step from the landing creaked, and she turned to scold her mother. "You shouldn't have climbed the steps again. They're too steep."

"I managed them all right," Greg said wryly.

"Oh! It's you!" she said, shocked.

His hair was longer and more unruly than it had been the last time she'd seen him, and his cheeks and chin were shadowed by the bristly beginnings of a beard. The London Fog raincoat, hanging open over a navy sweater and slacks, looked slept in.

"That's not a very warm welcome for a weary traveler."

"No, I suppose it isn't."

"Do you want to know how long it's taken me to get here from Oskaloosa, Iowa?"

"No." She was squashing the empty ribbon box in both hands.

"You probably don't want to know why I was there."

"You were thinking of building a restaurant there?"

He shook his head, frowning with narrowed eyes. "Eggs."

"Eggs?" She was having a hard time remaining hostile. He looked exhausted.

104

"Millions of them for my Midwest operations."

"Don't you have buyers to scout around for staples?"

"Sure, dozens of them."

"Then why try to do everything yourself?" She was still sitting by her desk, watching as he dropped down wearily on the edge of her bed.

"I like to keep busy. It looks like you do too." He gestured at the card table set up to hold stacks of papers.

"My book is going well." She didn't say it was nearly done; that would make her seem available.

"I'm sure it is."

Was she imagining the sarcasm in his voice?

The door buzzer was a welcome interruption. "My mother's going out."

"I thought she was expecting someone. She opened the door before I even buzzed. She sure does look pretty tonight," he said with a yawn.

"Yes, well, I need to see her before she leaves. Come on."

She sprinted down the stairs, expecting him to follow her out of her bedroom. But no footsteps echoed behind her. Martha hadn't seen her mother look so beautiful since the accident, and wondered if it was the date with Carl or Greg's return that had put the sparkle back in her mother's eyes. After exchanging a few words with her mother's escort—a thin, erect man with steel-gray hair and a winning smile—she wished them a good time and then went into the kitchen, thinking she could entice Greg downstairs with the offer of a meal. Whatever reason Greg had for being there, she didn't want to talk to him in her bedroom.

There was more than half of a chicken pie left from the previous evening. She could grate some cabbage for a quick salad, using a vinegar and cream dressing she'd tested for the cookbook. There were tart shells in the freezer ready to bake; she could slice the last of the winter's apples and make a quick dessert.

What was she thinking! Nervously biting her lower lip, she was torn between ordering Greg out of the house and throwing herself into his arms. Had he come because he cared about her, or did he still hope to sell her on taking his job?

There was one more immediate question: What was he doing in her bedroom?

Deliberately treading on the noisiest spots on the stairs, she gave him ample warning of her arrival. Stretched out on her bed in his raincoat, he didn't stir when she softly said his name. He'd kicked off his loafers and she couldn't bring herself to wake him. Instead she covered him with a spare quilt from her closet shelf. His deep breathing, lightly laced with snores, told her he might sleep for hours.

The spicy scent of cinnamon and cloves still lingered in the kitchen, although her tarts had been cooling for several hours. The kitchen table was set with her mother's wedding china, eggshell white plates with gold rims, and a cutwork linen tablecloth made by some forgotten great-great-aunt. She envied Greg his hours of oblivion. Thoughts churned around in her mind, denying her even the relaxation of reading a book or magazine.

Why was he there?

She heated the chicken pie, added dressing to the shredded cabbage, and decided he was going to have a late-night supper then leave, whether he liked it or not. Her mother would be home by midnight and he certainly wasn't spending the night, not in her bed.

He didn't respond at all to her voice. Leaning over him

106

warily, she touched his shoulder, jostling it just a bit when he showed no signs of waking.

"Greg, you've got to get up!"

Hurting because he looked so vulnerable and lovable, she ran the backs of her fingers over his bristly cheek, wanting so desperately to kiss him that she felt weepy.

"Terrible, isn't it?" He reached up sleepily and pulled her toward him.

"Your beard?"

"No, wanting someone you're not sure about."

Their kiss awoke a sweet longing in each of them. His beard was prickly but his mouth was softly devouring. She buried her fingers in his hair, feeling his hands caressing her back.

"I fixed dinner for you." At this moment she wanted to please him, not feed him.

"I'm not hungry for food." He kissed her again, showing her where his needs did lie.

They didn't hear the car that stopped in front of the house, but the front door buzzer was impossible to ignore.

"Who could that be?" he murmured.

Who indeed? "My mother!"

Neither woman carried a front door key; for some reason Fleury had summoned her to the street entrance instead of going through the passageway to the courtyard.

Martha didn't bother to check in the dresser mirror; she knew her hair was mussed and the skin around her mouth probably looked irritated from rubbing against Greg's whiskers. She had to answer the door; she couldn't leave her mother out on the street.

"I saw the downstairs lights on . . ." her mother began, becoming a little flustered when she saw how uneasy her daughter looked. "It's raining a little. I remembered how you fell when the flagstones were wet. Otherwise I would've gone to the back and used my key."

Martha started to tell her mother it didn't matter, but the words died in her throat when she followed her mother's gaze to the stairway.

"Greg, you're still here. What a nice surprise. I was afraid I wouldn't have a chance to visit with you."

"I was just washing up," Greg said quickly, gesturing toward the bathroom on the second floor. He made a show of gallantry by helping Fleury with her luminous silver rain cape. Thanks to years of scouring secondhand shops, her mother could dress for any occasion with dramatic flair. In old tan cords and a red flannel shirt laundered to a threadbare pink, Martha felt like Cinderella welcoming her stepmother home from the ball.

"Did you have a good time?" she asked.

"Marvelous! I had to sit most of the time, of course, but Carl was so attentive. I felt like a queen!"

"That's nice. Do you want something to eat with us? I made apple tarts."

"Oh, no, there was a marvelous buffet. I couldn't eat a bite."

"Marvelous," Martha mumbled, deciding that her mother was a bit too gushy this evening.

"Join us for a cup of coffee?" Greg asked.

"I'd love to!" Fleury thumped ahead of them into the kitchen, using her cane like a royal mace.

Greg pulled back a chair and seated her mother with courtly flourishes; Martha wished she'd go to bed.

"I like your dress," he said, complimenting Fleury's pink silk.

"We haven't seen you in some time," Fleury remarked.

"My loss," Greg said glibly, seating himself.

The chicken pie was edible, but not the succulent masterpiece it had been the night before. Greg ate two tarts and made her mother giggle like a schoolgirl.

"Won't you need to find a hotel room?" Martha finally asked.

"No, John and Rhonda gave me a key so I can use one of the kid's rooms."

She felt even more disgruntled knowing he'd gone to see his friends first. What was he doing in Alexandria? Her mother wasn't going to bed until she found out!

"Have you been on a buying trip for your firm, Greg?" Fleury asked.

"I'm selling this trip," he said, giving Martha a look that she understood: if she didn't tell her mother the truth, he would.

"Greg has an idea that I might be able to work for him," she said very tentatively.

"Doing what?" Her mother wasn't feigning her puzzled frown.

"You might call it promotional work," Martha explained, "but I'm pretty sure it's not right for me."

"You're highly qualified," Greg argued.

Martha's protest came out as a snort; she couldn't believe he'd use her mother as a lever against her.

"Qualified for what?" Fleury asked.

"To be a mascot for his new chain of restaurants," Martha said. "You know, like the giant chicken or the hamburger clown."

"Oh, wouldn't you need an actor for that sort of thing?" Fleury was a good actress herself, but she didn't quite manage to conceal her shock.

"It wouldn't be anything like that," Greg said quickly, glaring at Martha for an instant. "I want to name my new line Martha's Inns and serve colonial-style food. I was hoping your daughter would help me develop the menu and act as our spokesperson."

This obviously sounded more reasonable to Fleury, but she picked up on the discord between them, wisely removing herself from the argument. "I'm more tired than I thought. I haven't been out very much since my accident. You will excuse me, won't you, Greg?"

"You didn't have to do that!" Martha said when her mother was out of hearing on the second floor.

"You never mentioned it to her!" he accused her just as angrily. "Maybe you were afraid your own mother would think it's a great idea."

"She didn't!"

"Only because you started talking about clowns and chickens!"

He stood and walked to the aged brick fireplace, staring moodily at the blackened interior of the open hearth. Less weary-looking since his nap, he still slouched, standing with both hands crowded into the side pockets of his slacks.

"Why did you come here?" she asked, holding her breath, dreading to hear that he'd only come to repeat his job offer.

"Don't you know?" He looked at her over his shoulder.

"I didn't think I'd ever see you again." Her voice was husky as she spoke the painful truth and she couldn't face him, instead awkwardly keeping busy by clearing the table.

"Stop that." He walked over to her.

"I need to put the salad in—"

"That's not what I mean! Stop pretending you don't know why I'm really here."

There was nothing she could say without revealing

110

how acutely she longed for him, how desperately she wanted to be in his arms again.

Taking a tentative little half-step toward him, her soul was revealed in the depths of deep blue eyes sparkling now as tiny tears threatened to escape.

Just being held was enough for the moment. His arms circled her back, letting the warmth of protectiveness flow through her. Groaning like a man who doesn't want to wake up and leave a cozy bed, he held her even tighter, pressing his lips against her forehead.

"Greg—"

"No talk."

He made it impossible to disobey by covering her mouth with his, drawing her lips between his, kissing her with slow, heart-stopping intensity.

"I was starving for that," he murmured, leading her into the dimly-lit living room and pulling her onto his lap on the couch.

"Wow!" He shook his head and buried his face against her throat.

"Am I that heavy?" she teased, wanting to be held until the end of time.

His hair was unruly against her cheek and his bristles rasped against the soft skin of her neck, making her squirm and inch her fingers over his chin.

"I know, you don't deserve a porcupine," he said, bestowing a genuinely friendly smile on her for the first time since his arrival.

It's fine as long as you're my porcupine, she wanted to say; instead she ran the tip of her finger over the tenderly soft skin under his eyes.

"Men are funny creatures," she mused, letting his dark, spiky lashes tickle her nose. "All bristle and bone in some places, so soft in others."

111

"I don't mind you knowing my soft spots." He set out to demonstrate how deliciously slippery and yielding the inner flesh of his lips was, unbuttoning her worn flannel shirt to confirm that she didn't bother with a bra when she slaved over the typewriter all day. Easing her flat on her back, he knelt on the floor and leaned over her, cupping one breast, gently suckling it until ripples of pleasure made her moan and clutch his head.

"We can't go to your room," he said unhappily.

"We can't go to Rhonda and John's either," she said.

"I'll call a hotel."

"It's too late," she protested.

"We have so much to talk about." He brushed his lips against her bare midriff, resting his hands in a place calculated to push her over the brink, into a frenzy.

She didn't want to talk! He slid his fingers under her waistband, stroking her tummy until she felt overwhelmed by the delicious sensations his touch was producing.

The thud of Fleury's cane was unmistakable on the bare boards of the second-floor hallway. Martha shot up, buttoning her shirt as she did, laughing nervously when she realized her mother wasn't coming downstairs.

"She probably can't sleep after her big evening. She's going to get a book from the shelves in my dad's office."

"My sex life hasn't been this complicated since high school," he said with a sigh.

Her life had never been so complicated!

"I'll be here early tomorrow morning." He seemed resigned to leaving for the night.

"You can have breakfast here."

"No, we'll go someplace where we can talk. I rented a car at the airport."

112

"Talk about what?" Much as she tried, she couldn't suppress her suspicions about his motive for visiting her.

Standing now, he took both of her hands in his. "I brought a contract with me. No, don't say anything." He touched her lips with two fingers to silence her. "At least give me a fair hearing."

"I won't change my mind," she insisted, miserable because she wanted to say things that would make him happy.

"We'll see tomorrow."

He landed a quick peck on her clenched lips, reclaimed his raincoat, and left, leaving her in the doorway staring out at the wet brick walk, shiny under a misty rain, and receding taillights.

In tailored navy slacks, a gray tweed sweater-vest, and a fresh white oxford cloth blouse, she looked ready to face the day but her spirits drooped. Greg ignored everything she said; he had a contract ready for her signature and saying no another time was going to be an ordeal.

When he came for her, she readily agreed to breakfast in a hotel dining room. A public place where the other patrons were strangers seemed the best setting for their confrontation. If she didn't care so much, if she had it in her to reject Greg along with his contract, she wouldn't dread listening to his arguments.

The morning sun was bright, promising one of the nicest days in months. Martha hardly needed the raincoat she automatically grabbed.

They selected breakfast from a buffet table, slowly ate scrambled eggs, hash browns, fresh fruit, and thick slices of toasted whole wheat, then lingered over strong hot coffee, enjoying their companionship, putting off the time to talk business.

"Let's walk," she suggested.

"After you read the contract. Carefully."

This was the first time she'd seen him with a briefcase. He extracted one copy of the document his lawyers had prepared, handing it to her. Their eyes met and she wished he wasn't so appealing. In a subdued brown plaid sport coat with a tan shirt and a coordinated brown tie, he looked businesslike and dignified and terribly sexy.

"First let me tell you," he said, "I turned your recipes over to my research staff. Their report made me respect your skills even more. We'll be able to utilize several of them. I brought this for you."

The check was made out by his company treasurer; the amount staggered her.

"I didn't get this much as a cookbook advance." That was the understatement of her career.

"You're dealing with a profit-making operation now."

"It's still too much."

"I can't possibly pay you enough for the inspiration you've given me. Before I met you, I was just fishing for ideas. I was bored with my whole corporation. You've given me new enthusiasm. I can't put a price tag on that."

"I haven't done that much." His compliment confused her; he was greatly overrating her contribution.

Keeping her feet on solid ground was almost impossible when Greg turned the full force of his charm on her. She clutched the sheaf of pages, trying to concentrate on the words dancing in front of her eyes.

"If there's anything that isn't clear," he said after a few minutes of silence, "I'll be glad to explain."

Nothing was clear! She read all the whereas and here-after clauses without absorbing anything, but not because she couldn't understand legal terminology. What she

114

couldn't comprehend was Greg's purpose. He was offering sums of money that seemed like the pot of gold at the end of the rainbow. What was he really buying? She felt as if her soul was up for grabs in his long, confusing contract.

"There are three important specifications: your endorsement, your active participation in promotions, and the exclusive use of your name."

"It's like signing my life over to you."

"Not quite." His smile was meant to reassure but it made her shiver nervously.

"It's too much. I don't know how to handle it."

"I won't let you sign without having a lawyer of your own go over the wording."

"That's very fair, but—"

"There's nothing in the language that contradicts anything I've told you."

"Greg, I'm not worried about the contract. It's the job! I don't think it's for me."

"Maybe I'm asking too much," he said slowly.

She could agree with that!

"After all, you don't know anything about the way I run my business." It seemed to cost him something to admit this.

"No, I don't."

"Have you ever eaten at a Turkey Haven?"

"No, but I've passed one or two on trips."

"That's not quite the same," he said dryly. "The colonial restaurants will be a different style, but the organization behind them will be the same. I think you need to see how I do things."

"I'm not sure what you mean."

"A tour! I like to visit some of the franchises every year

115

to see how they're being run. Why not now? You can come with me."

"I don't know, Greg."

"I should've thought of it sooner. We'll drive north, I think, at least as far as New Jersey. The district manager there has had some problems."

"I haven't said I'd go!"

"Let's walk while we talk about it."

There was warmth in the sunlight, but the air was invigoratingly cool. Later the tourists would come in droves along with the muggy heat of summer, but this day was perfect. Walking arm in arm with Greg was wonderfully stimulating; Martha almost convinced herself that his tour idea was plausible.

"Being with me on this trip, darling, you'll see I'm not trying to rope you into anything that isn't in your best interest too."

She glowed under his term of endearment, loving the way his voice caressed the word *darling*.

They were walking in Market Square across from the red-brick Victorian city hall, but Greg wasn't interested in sightseeing today. He guided her to one of the benches and took her hand in both of his.

"There's no reason why we can't leave today, is there?" he urged.

After anxiously rehearsing in her mind all the reasons not to work for him, she was dumbfounded by his new proposal.

"I don't know what to say."

"I don't see how you can turn down the job without seeing how I operate. You're going to see crack management, clean kitchens, wholesome food." He laughed at himself but didn't give up. "What can you lose by looking?"

"Time."

"Not much—a few days, a week. It'll be time spent with me."

"Yes, I know."

"Will it be so terrible, being with me? I want to be with you very much."

It was all she could do to sit and calmly listen to him. She felt like dancing in the square, leaping from bench to bench, celebrating the promise in his voice!

"You want me to see your business firsthand." She was stalling for time, saying inane things because it put off the moment of decision.

"With me."

"Yes, with you."

If he took her in his arms again, she wouldn't be able to refuse him anything. She was at war with herself, wanting Greg and not wanting his job.

"Let's go back," he said, standing and reaching for her hand.

"No, wait."

"You aren't going to say no to this?" He sounded worried and sat beside her again.

"I have to know," she said. "This is just a business trip, isn't it?"

"Is that what you want it to be?"

"That's what it has to be!"

If she stayed in his room, slept in his bed, she'd never be able to refuse his job offer.

"You're a hard bargainer." He didn't smile.

"I can't go otherwise."

What would happen after she signed the contract, if she did? Would that be the end of them? Would he consider his mission accomplished?

"I see."

He stood and walked a few yards across the brick pathway, keeping his back toward her.

"Greg?" She didn't like talking to his back.

"Okay, you have a deal." He turned and smiled, but his smile didn't dispel the disappointment in his eyes. "A business trip. Separate rooms."

"I don't want to be gone too long. My mother still doesn't drive or get out to shop. She has friends who will look in or run errands but—"

"Yes, that's fine," he interrupted impatiently. "I'd better tell the Van Looses they've lost a house guest."

"And I'll pack. It won't take me long."

Back at the house without Greg, she showed the contract to her mother, fidgeting impatiently while Fleury thoroughly read it.

"I'm sure Carl would go over this for you," she said.

"Mother, I'm almost certain I don't want to sign it."

"It is a bit ambiguous in parts, especially about promoting. Greg could have you wearing a chicken costume. But he's certainly offering a large amount of money."

"He wants me to visit some of his Turkey Havens before I make a decision."

"I suppose that's a good idea."

"You think I should?"

She'd counted on her mother to argue her out of going!

"Well, it sounds reasonable. You wouldn't accept any other job without investigating first."

"I'm thinking of not accepting."

Fleury looked at the contract again, obviously a little shaken by the generosity of the terms.

"That has to be your decision," her mother said matter-of-factly.

An hour later Greg's car drove up, and Martha left her house with more misgivings than hope.

CHAPTER SEVEN

A man reveals his true self when he drives an automobile. This was one of Martha's pet theories. She expected Greg to drive fast, take chances cutting in and out of traffic lanes, and generally be aggressive on the highway.

She was pleasantly surprised. Instead of being heavy-footed and short on patience, he drove at a moderate speed, was so safety conscious he reminded her to buckle up, and treated other drivers with courtesy even when they didn't deserve it. The short drive to the environs of Baltimore should've been pleasurable, but the business nature of the trip made both of them behave like wary strangers.

They visited two Turkey Havens, eating lunch at the second; her turkey à la king on baked potato was rather good. Greg was critical of the deep-fried turkey chunks but the one she tried was moist on the inside with crispy batter on the outside.

The managers treated Greg like a ruling potentate. The same local man owned both franchises, and he was hastily summoned to meet them at their second stop.

The kitchens were immaculately clean—even during the noon rush—the employees seemed cheerful, and the decor was done in restful shades of maize and blue with carpeting and partitioned booths.

"I'm impressed," she said when they were back in the

rented car, "but I don't think I need to see more Turkey Havens."

"You agreed to a short tour."

"Yes, but—"

"We've only begun," he said sternly.

Seeing him in action didn't make her reluctant to be with him. On the contrary, she admired the way he handled people, eliciting the information he wanted without making them feel threatened. He stood tall in his own kingdom without lording it over anyone.

The car was beginning to seem too small for the two of them as they followed the Kennedy Memorial to Wilmington. Not a moment passed when she wasn't totally aware of him. His hold on the steering wheel was sure but not tense and she found herself remembering against her better judgment how it felt to have those fingers trail over her flesh, leaving her weak with desire.

Greg was suffering too. She could see it in the grim set of his jaw and his tightly pursed lips. To be so close without touching was an ordeal. Martha wanted very much to go home.

"We'll have dinner at a Turkey Haven?" she asked.

"Unless you'd rather visit the franchise, then go somewhere fancier."

"No." The last thing she wanted was to linger over candlelight at a table for two, not when she was determined to spend the night alone.

They dined pretending to be customers; Greg occasionally liked to check out the service that way. Her turkey salad wasn't bad, but it was beginning to seem like the week after Thanksgiving.

"Aren't you afraid people will get tired of turkey?"

The question didn't please him. "Why should they? It

120

tastes delicious, and people are getting more and more health conscious."

Greg had called ahead from Alexandria that morning; two motel rooms were waiting for them. Before he went inside to register, she gave it one more try.

"I really don't need to see more. I'm convinced," she said, willing to plead if it would free her from this no-win trip with him. "There isn't any reason for me to look at Turkey Havens in New Jersey tomorrow."

"You agreed," he reminded her.

Their rooms were adjoining. He placed one key on her palm, lingering over it longer than necessary.

"Let me take your bag in."

Her antique Samsonite looked like an overweight matron beside his streamlined lightweight modern bag. It was in remarkably good shape, but forty years ago suitcases had been made for sturdiness; hers weighed about a hundred pounds tonight but she insisted on carrying it herself.

Greg stood in the doorway watching, making her feel like she was doing a feminist number on him: proving that she had beaucoup muscles.

"I thought we'd get started early. Do you want breakfast here?" he asked, his voice totally devoid of friendliness.

"Whatever you like."

"Whatever?" He arched one brow and took a step into the room.

"Whatever you want for breakfast is fine with me!" She wasn't in any mood to play games. Touring Turkey Havens took a lot out of a person.

The next morning he was cross, preferring the newspaper to her conversation.

"I know now you're not a morning person," she complained.

"Do you?" He regarded her with a cold unblinking stare.

"I'm sorry I mentioned it!"

The rainy season wasn't over in New Jersey. Her feet and the legs of her slacks got soaked dashing through a puddle on her way into the third Turkey Haven of the day. She squished around with him on a tour of the facility, sneezing so loudly by the salad table that he suggested she change into dry clothes.

"I think it's the pepper in the salad dressing."

His glare told her not to be silly. "I'll bring your suitcase in."

"No!" It didn't seem at all dignified to drag a hundred-pound suitcase into a fast food restaurant.

"You're soaked." His quiet scorn made her feel like an uninvited guest at dinner time.

"I'll go out and get what I need—some dry slacks and shoes."

"I'm willing to help you."

His tone of voice forced her to say "No, thank you."

If she rummaged through her suitcase while it was still inside the trunk of the car, even her raincoat would soak through. She reluctantly lifted it out, setting it on the ground, then opened one of the back doors and wrestled it onto the seat. At least that way she could sort out what she needed in a dry place.

With dry shoes, hose, and slacks folded into a bundle under her raincoat, she made a dash back to the restaurant, remembering when she was changing in the rest room that she hadn't relocked the car. She wasn't too worried; there couldn't be much of a market for a forty-year-old suitcase left on a backseat.

122

Her reward for a day of trudging around to Turkey Havens was dinner at a Chinese restaurant. She was ready to order dinner for six with egg rolls until Greg noticed that the back door on her side wasn't locked.

Where her suitcase had been, there was a damp-looking spot on the upholstery.

"My suitcase is gone!"

"What do you mean?"

"It was on the back seat."

He looked skeptical. "Maybe you've forgotten putting it back in the trunk."

It was only a minor triumph when he opened the rear and confirmed the theft. She was furious at him for doubting her word.

"Your insurance will probably cover it."

Her faith in insurance policies had diminished considerably since her mother's difficulties, and she could ill-afford to lose two of her best pairs of slacks. The only good thing was that now he'd have to take her home.

"We might as well start back to Alexandria right now," she suggested hopefully.

"No way will I drive at night in this rain. Come on, you'll feel better after some Cantonese cuisine."

"I can't possibly continue with this tour without clothes."

He laughed off her objection. "We'll stop at a shopping mall tomorrow."

"I don't want to buy new clothes." She couldn't afford to, not with a gigantic doctor's bill still hanging over her mother's head.

"I want to buy you something for coming with me." She heard the first note of tenderness in his voice since they'd started the tour.

This time their rooms were on opposite sides of a green and gold carpeted corridor.

"I am sorry about your suitcase," he said, lingering outside her door before she opened it.

"It was my own fault for not locking the car." Admitting she was dumb didn't make her feel better.

"I think," he said slowly, "that if I don't kiss you good night, I'm going to come out of my lonesome room in the morning babbling like a maniac."

"That would be terrible!" She took a little half-step closer, not exactly rushing into his arms but certainly not putting up a struggle.

He stepped back a bit, making her feel like the aggressor.

"When I registered, I saw some vending machines near the lobby. Why don't I go down and see if there's a toothbrush for you?"

"I'd appreciate one."

A half hour later she thought she'd have to forget about brushing her teeth that night. Greg had been gone long enough to make three trips to the lobby.

Was there anything emptier than a motel room with two double beds and one single person? She turned on the TV, kicked off her shoes, and propped up two pillows against the headboard. Even the paperback romance she'd brought as entertainment had been in the stolen suitcase.

The program playing seemed to be one long gunfight, but before she could change stations a commercial break came she was very much interested in. Turkey Havens was announcing a big nationwide giveaway contest.

"Just pick up your Mr. Turkey lotto card at any Turkey Haven," a bouncy, feathered creature somewhat resembling a fowl was telling the television audience.

124

She stared with distaste at the big, ugly bird and listened with greater disdain to the list of fabulous prizes that Turkey Haven customers could win.

What kind of contests would Greg authorize to promote Martha's Inns? How about a trip to historical Alexandria, she thought ruefully, with a personal tour by Martha Graves. She didn't think the Turkey Havens' promotion was necessarily his brainchild, but using her was his idea.

She was still disgruntled when Greg's soft knock summoned her to the door. She turned off the TV on her way to answer.

"I had to find a drugstore." His hair was damp because there'd been no letup in the steady drizzle outside.

"You didn't need to—"

"Here. Toothpaste, toothbrush, tissues, comb, hairbrush, lipstick—I hope you like Rose Blush. And perfume."

"I can get along without perfume."

"I like a sweet scent." He hung his raincoat on the rack beside hers.

"You didn't need to buy all this."

"Just say thank you and forget it." He smiled, walking across the room to the bed where she'd been sitting with pillows behind her back.

"Thank you and good night, Greg."

"You're forgetting."

"What?"

"A good-night kiss, my reward for two days of perfect behavior."

"You've been crabby! I don't call that perfect behavior."

"Have I annoyed you?" He was standing so close she could almost feel his body heat radiating toward her.

125

"Yes—no."

"Yes, I have, but no, you don't want to admit it."

Backing up until her legs touched the edge of the bed, she answered sharply. "You promised nothing would happen!"

"I agreed to separate rooms. I couldn't possibly promise to stop wanting you." His voice was low and serious.

"This trip isn't accomplishing anything! I insist you take me home tomorrow."

"I have to meet with a district manager before I go back."

"Then I'll take a bus."

"I won't buy your ticket."

It was a cheap shot, and he had enough grace to blush. Unfortunately she didn't have enough money with her to get all the way home. She'd left most of her pocket money with her mother to take care of little expenses that came up and his check was lying uncashed on her desk.

"I'm serious about wanting you to stay with me," he said unrepentantly.

"There's no point in it!"

"There's no point in kissing you either, but there's nothing I want more than to do just that."

"Greg . . ." Her knees were weakening as quickly as her common sense was deserting her. "Hold me," she whispered, even though she knew she should throw him out of her room.

He held her in his arms, tucking her head under his chin.

"What is this business of two rooms?" he challenged softly, stroking her hair away from her forehead.

"I don't want to be . . ." She meant to say "swept away," but changed her mind. If he knew how she felt,

126

he'd have a powerful weapon with which he could coax her into signing the contract.

"Come here." He sat down on the edge of the bed and pulled her down beside him. "You're right to keep me at arm's length."

"Am I?" If she was right, why was she so miserable?

"I've always avoided mixing my business and personal interests. It makes good sense."

"Then we're all business?"

"No, damn it! That's the trouble!"

He sounded as confused as she felt.

"Greg—"

"No, let me say something. I'm determined to have you involved in Martha's Inns."

"I don't think—"

"Let me finish! It's the best idea I've had in years; even my management team thinks so, and I don't hire yes-men. But when I'm with you, I forget about restaurants and contracts and all of it."

She took a deep breath, sure that this was the part she wanted to hear.

"I'm tremendously attracted to you, Martha."

She bit her lower lip in disappointment. "Tremendously attracted" was no substitute for saying he loved her.

He touched her cheek with the backs of his fingers, studying her profile in silence for a moment.

"More than that," he said softly, holding her hand on his lap and stroking the inside of her wrist. "You're on my mind constantly."

He was scoring points; she could feel little tingles of desire traveling up and down her back.

"With you I will keep business and pleasure separate," he said.

"I don't know how you can." She didn't know how to pretend that this enchanting man wasn't disrupting her life.

"I'll start by not mentioning the contract again until you do."

"That's a big start." She was sure she'd never bring the subject up again. "Do you mean never, ever?"

"Yes, never, ever."

He was so close she could feel his warm breath caressing her ear.

"Darling." He slid his fingers under her chin, turning her face to his. "Let me do something."

His voice was hoarse with passion and she trembled at his vague request, afraid to turn her imagination loose on the possibilities. What did she really know about Greg, except that he had devastating charm and dark, intense eyes which seemed to see through her? In spite of all that was between them, she was afraid of being in over her head.

"What?" She sounded scared.

"Nothing sinister." He laughed softly, unnerving her again by seemingly reading her mind. "Let me brush your hair."

Instinctively touching her head, she realized that the rain had made her hair curl into tight, unruly ringlets. "It's a mess," she said without thinking.

"No, it's beautiful. I love the streaks of gold that show when it's brushed."

He didn't wait for her answer. He took a brush from the drugstore bag, and standing beside her, pressing his thigh and torso against her half-turned shoulder, gently worked the brush through the short locks on the sides, around to the long, snarled fall in back. He brushed her hair into a shiny halo around her face, all the while making her aware of the lean hardness of his hipbone, the long, firm line of his thigh.

No one but a hairdresser had brushed her hair since she was ten. She felt cherished.

"That's better." He rested his hands on the back of her neck, gently massaging away the tension until she felt light-headed and almost giddy with longing.

She wasn't sure what to say to a man who'd just made a ritual of brushing her hair. "Thank you," was all she managed.

"You're very welcome."

Standing, walking restlessly across the confined space of the room, she groped for some distraction. "I saw your ad on TV."

"What's that?" He was watching her, too absorbed in his own thoughts to hear what she said.

"Your big giveaway ad. I saw it on TV. Mr. Turkey. The Caribbean cruise."

"Do you really want to talk about that?" He followed her.

"No, I suppose not."

Retreating, she'd stepped between the two beds; now he blocked her way. For a panicky moment she thought of scrambling across a bed to escape, but, of course, that wasn't what she wanted. She faced him squarely, letting all that she felt show on her face.

"Martha."

His husky whisper gave her goose bumps, and she hugged her arms across her chest, burning with anticipation as he slowly moved toward her.

This was her last chance to insist that he go to his own room; she blew it. His lips met hers in a kiss that went on and on and on, washing away all the obstacles between them. She wanted to be his; she'd deal with the consequences later, much later.

Greg dropped his jacket on the one unrumpled blue and yellow floral bedspread, then slid her white cotton blouse from her shoulders, tossing it beside his garment.

The front of his shirt was too thin to completely conceal the dark hair on his chest. Moving her hands over the sheer cotton was nearly as exciting as touching his flesh. Starting at the top she slowly unbuttoned his shirt, kissing his furry skin. She was committed to whatever would happen; she could never blame him for violating their agreement.

His fingers undid her buttons hastily, tearing the last one off in his eagerness to rip the blouse free of her slacks.

"Sorry." He smiled apologetically. "It is your only one, isn't it?" He kissed her on the mouth before she could reply. Then his lips worked their way down over her neck to her breasts. As his tongue teased each rosy tip, he pulled down the front zipper on her slacks. It threatened to stick, but he worked it downward with magical fingers, lingering on the silky surface of her panties, gently probing until she moaned softly in his ear.

"I should go now," he teased without moving, making her wonder if she was trafficking with a devil who had superhuman powers to arouse her.

"Could you do that?" She leaned her head back to look into his eyes, which were bright with passion.

"I don't think my legs can carry me as far as the door."

His body was lean and well-proportioned; she couldn't get enough of touching him. The silkiness under his arms delighted her, and she traced his rib cage until it gave way to a slender waistline and lean, firm hips. Stepping

130

free of her slacks which were tangled around her ankles, she slid her hand lower to touch the tab on his fly.

"Go ahead," he whispered.

With trembling fingers she unzipped his trousers and pulled them down. On her knees she peeled off his navy cotton briefs, sliding her hands back up the length of his legs, loving the fuzziness that was hard bone and tight muscles.

Sitting on the edge of the bed, he kicked off his trousers and briefs and pulled her into his arms, kissing her with a force that warned her he couldn't hold back forever. What was happening between them was more than a game of lovemaking. They were tapping the deepest wellsprings of their sensuality, probing passions that were threatening to engulf them both.

Pushing aside the covers, he stretched out and pressed her body against his, moving his legs against and between hers, covering her breasts with hot, seeking kisses, rolling and twisting and caressing, tangling into a lovers' knot as their mouths devoured and their frenzy heightened.

His hands were heavy on the swells of her hips; then he burrowed his palms under the warm flesh of her bottom, arching his body over hers, lifting her to meet his thrust. At first she was all tension; he was all power. Then, without conscious thought, she began responding with her whole body, growing first limp and languid, then unbearably aroused, wanting him, wanting Greg, wanting all that he was.

"So wonderful . . ."

She barely heard his dazed words. He shifted his length, resting his cheek against the curve of her hipbone, stroking the skin stretched taut over her tummy, crooning sweet words that she was etching on her memory.

When she awoke, his lips were grazing the backs of her

131

knees, sending a message that she wasn't inclined to resist.

The next time they both woke up, a bright sliver of sunlight lay across their legs; the morning came into the room through a narrow opening where the heavy drapes didn't quite meet.

She dozed again while he showered then got up when she heard the water shut off. Her hair was a mass of tangled curls again but she felt as if she were glowing with vitality. Greg's shirt was lying in a heap on the unused bed and she slipped into it, leaving it open in front as she stood by the mirror brushing her hair.

Greg came up behind her, still damp and naked from the shower, and slipped his hand under the shirt, giving her little love squeezes until she turned and fell into his arms, kissing his freshly-shaved face.

"I change my mind," he said seriously.

"About what?" She nipped the end of his nose with her teeth.

"Perfume. You couldn't possibly smell any nicer."

Eventually she showered and shampooed, too radiant to mind that her suitcase was gone and her clothes weren't fresh.

"While I meet with my district manager, you can do some shopping," Greg said, insisting that she take some cash from him.

"I won't take money except as a loan." She could cash his check for the recipes and pay him back as soon as she got home.

"Don't be silly. Think what I'll save with us sharing a room."

She knew that's what they'd do for the rest of the trip, but hearing him say it put a damper on her mood. She didn't want to be his traveling companion or his playmate. The only relationship she really wanted with any man was a permanent one; "eternally yours" and "happily ever after" meant a great deal to her. Greg seemed oblivious to ideas like these. In the throes of passion, when he literally showered compliments and endearments on her, he never slipped in a single "I love you."

By the time he left her at a shopping mall, she was morose about the future. She couldn't imagine ever forgetting Greg or changing in the way she felt about him, but somewhere he had a whole life of his own that didn't include her. How could she become part of that life? Did he want to share more than a week of glorious lovemaking?

After buying some underwear and other essentials in a big chain department store, she tried on blouses, selecting a tailored white and a pale blue to wear with the slacks left to her. She could finish Greg's tour with what she had, but did she want to?

The suit was in the window of a small, expensive women's wear shop—a red silk-blend suit with a skirt that looked slinky and sexy on the mannequin. Could she wear something like that?

A three-way mirror told her she could. The skirt hugged her hips and the jacket had a nipped-in look at the waistline. With a white jersey top cut like an especially revealing tank top, Martha saw an exciting dynamic woman reflected in the mirror. Would Greg like her this way? She fluffed her hair out and told the salesperson she'd wear the suit. There was just enough of Greg's cash left to pay for it.

Tomorrow she might be guilt-stricken over her extravagant purchase, but for once she'd followed an impulse in buying. The only thing that mattered in her life right now was being close to Greg. For his sake, she didn't want to be her old practical self.

His reaction was all the reward she needed.

"Never wear anything but red."

"That means I'll have to wear this all the time."

"Do it." He nuzzled her ear and quickly kissed the lobe.

Her reckless new self wasn't quite ready for displays of affection in a crowded shopping mall.

"Behave yourself!"

"I never have any fun that way."

They didn't visit anymore Turkey Havens that day or the next. Greg found a beguiling country inn that had just opened for the season and secured a room with one double bed, a thick down quilt, and two dormer windows overlooking a countryside just beginning to show new green growth.

The inn served breakfast and dinner in a series of little parlors George Washington could've visited. They missed breakfast but dined on Yankee pot roast in front of a glowing fireplace.

"You're eating red meat," Martha teased.

"I need extra strength."

The dark circles had disappeared from under his eyes; he looked younger and happier than she'd ever seen him. Why didn't he say the things that needed to be said? Why couldn't he see that they belonged together forever?

He kept his word about the contract; not even a hint about it came from him, but Martha brooded over it whenever her attention strayed from the wonder of being with Greg. If she refused his job, would she see him again? He loved his business; how would he feel about her if she rejected it?

One of her pet theories held up through the wonderful

hours they spent together: nothing is ever perfect. If things are going too well, there's a setback just ahead. Unbridled happiness was a myth. Her own joy in Greg's company was balanced by growing apprehension about the future. Today he wanted nothing but her, but soon he'd remember his business, his obligations, and his plans for a new restaurant chain.

The second afternoon they napped in the four-poster bed, snuggled under the down guilt, waking to make leisurely love. Familiarity only fired their sensuality; she'd never be able to see or feel enough of his wonderfully strong, lithe body. She discovered she could be aroused by the most innocent touches: kisses on her elbow, strokes on the small of her back, caresses on her fine, slender ankles.

They didn't talk about leaving.

Dinner the second night wasn't a gourmet's delight; a new chef overcooked the sole and overseasoned the stuffing, but neither of them minded. In fact, they hardly noticed.

"I should call my mother tonight," she said, "and tell her when I'll be home."

She was more anxious to know than Fleury would be.

"I suppose I have to get back to work sometime."

He rubbed his chin on the side with the thin white scar, a habit of his when something was disturbing him. She hoped it was the prospect of being separated from her.

"You said your management people are highly qualified."

"Yes, but there are decisions only I can make."

He didn't mention Martha's Inns. Not once had he broken his word, but the question was often there in his eyes. Would she accept his offer? Did she dare risk losing him by refusing?

Greg was well into his thirties. He certainly must have had an active sex life before meeting her, but he was evasive about the women in his past. She wasn't even sure all the women in his life were part of his past. It wasn't logical to be jealous of rivals that might not exist, but fears in this direction were one more cloud on her present bliss.

"What should I tell my mother then?" she pressed.

"Let me think about it until morning. Is that too late to call her?"

"No, that's fine."

Greg fell asleep before she did. Standing in front of the window, she shivered and hugged herself. A nightgown hadn't been one of the necessities purchased on her trip to the mall. Greg, she now knew, never slept with a stitch of clothing. What would he think of her winter flannel pajamas? Probably not much, but did it matter? Would their affair last until next winter?

Greg was going to take her home soon; she sensed it in his evasiveness. He wanted to pretend that they could go on forever the way they were, but reality was intruding on him as well as on her.

He was waiting for her answer. Sooner or later she had to tell him her decision, but she didn't know what it would be. There was one question Greg could ask that would receive an unqualified yes, but he was mute on anything concerning the two of them. He wasn't tiring of her; in fact, the more they made love, the more eager both became. Why was he living from moment to moment without giving her any guarantees for the future?

When she finally crawled into bed again, her feet were so cold she woke Greg rubbing them against his calf. He knew the fastest way in the world to warm her but didn't seem to know the first thing about love or commitment or two people building a life together.

She fell asleep firmly convinced that her future depended on whether or not she signed Greg's contract. Snuggled against his back, she realized she was willing to do anything to remain a part of his life.

CHAPTER EIGHT

Her mother's line was busy. This wasn't unusual. Since the accident friends often called to help her pass the time. An hour later Martha found the busy signal annoying, and two hours later she was worried. Why was Fleury spending the whole morning on the phone?

Greg would soon return from another meeting with the district manager, and they planned to check out of the inn at noon. Impatient now, Martha sat by the phone in their room and kept dialing every minute or so until she was finally rewarded by a ring.

"Mother, I've been trying to call for hours."

"Well, it hasn't been an ordinary morning." There was none of the usual sparkle in her voice.

"What's wrong?"

"Nothing that we weren't expecting, but that doesn't make it any less disastrous."

"Mother, tell me!"

"That committee met, you know, about my accident insurance."

"The Peer Review Committee?"

"Yes. They completely agreed with the insurance company. They advised them not to pay my balance. I can't hate the doctor who made it possible for me to keep walking, but I just don't know how I'll manage the rest of his fee."

138

"It's our problem now?" Martha didn't pretend she wasn't upset. "We'll have to pay the rest of his bill?"

"I don't expect you to take the responsibility, dear. I'm going to look into selling the house, see what it's worth. Maybe we'd be better off in a nice little apartment, something easier to care for."

"No!" Martha was grimly emphatic. "You can't give up your only asset. We'll work something out."

"Carl's coming tonight to take me out for dinner. I thought I'd mention it to him. See what he thinks."

To Martha, lawyers meant more bills, even if the attorney in question was a friend. "Yes, well, we'll find a way to pay," she said.

"This is my problem. I don't want it to worry you," her mother insisted.

Martha didn't argue but she couldn't possibly turn her back on her only parent. Somehow, somewhere, she'd have to find a way to pay her mother's staggering debt.

When Greg came back she was wearing the red suit, trying to seem cheerful and untroubled.

"Are you ready to go?" He loosened his tie and unbuttoned his top shirt button. "I've done all I need to do here."

"We're going back to Alexandria?"

"I don't want to." He stepped close and brushed a kiss on her forehead. "But I have things to do."

He was keeping his promise by not mentioning his business. In a way it made her sad. He was avoiding any mention of the things that meant the most to him, and she didn't feel free to lay her problems on him. Their relationship didn't make it possible for her to accept any kind of offer from him to help with her mother's medical bill, and she was afraid that's just what he'd do.

139

"Are you sad about leaving here?" He lifted one of her hands to his cheek.

"It's been wonderful. I hate to see it end," she said wistfully.

"Me too." He kissed her fingers one by one, a tender gesture meant to lead nowhere.

"When will I see you again?" She asked this question as if her life depended on the answer.

"I honestly don't know." He didn't sound happy. "I'll have to call you."

"You don't 'have to.'"

"I didn't mean it that way."

"How did you mean it?" She was quibbling, being deliberately quarrelsome to disguise the fact that her heart was breaking.

"Only that I don't know what my schedule will be," he said.

She glanced around the spacious country room where they'd been so happy. Blue wildflowers were scattered on the cream wallpaper, and braided oval rugs made cheerful spots of color on the waxed floorboards. Afraid that they'd never return, she wanted to memorize every detail.

If Greg didn't love her, she'd live the rest of her life as an old maid. It was the first time she'd ever considered such an antiquated notion, but the truth behind it stunned her. Part of her would die if she couldn't be with the man she loved.

"Ready?" he asked, picking up the suitcase that now contained her things too.

"No." She wasn't ready to lose him. "I mean, can we talk for a few minutes?"

"Checkout time is noon. It's nearly that. Can't we talk in the car?"

140

By the time they reached it, she might change her mind.

"I want to talk about your contract."

"You've reconsidered?" The hope he managed to suppress in his voice showed in his eyes.

"I've decided to accept your proposal." It wasn't the one she wanted, but it was the only one he'd made.

"Darling, that's wonderful!" He grabbed her in a bear hug that swept her off her feet. "You don't know how happy that makes me!"

"I want to sign right now." She walked away to fish for a pen in her purse; now was no time to let him see her face.

"There's no big hurry. Remember, I want your attorney to read it over first."

"I trust you. There's no need."

"I didn't write the contract. My lawyers did, and they had my welfare in mind. I'd really feel better if you'd let someone look at it. That way if there's any question—"

"Greg, I want to sign it now." She had the pen in position between her thumb and fingers. "All three copies."

"First, tell me why you've decided in favor of it."

"Isn't it enough that I have?"

She'd never admit that fear of losing him was driving her to it. Nor did she want him to know that her mother needed money now more desperately than ever.

"I couldn't be happier about it, but my briefcase is in the trunk. Do you want to wait here while I get it?"

"No, I can sign in the car."

She did, affixing her signature on three copies of the contract without looking at any of them.

"You should reread it," he warned.

As a shrewd businessman he sounded disapproving,

but Martha could see the satisfaction written all over his face.

"I read it once. Is there some tricky clause I should know about?"

"Of course not. It's just a good habit to read before you sign anything."

She only shrugged and handed the sheaf of papers back to him.

"One copy is for you after I sign it." He took his own pen from an inner pocket of his jacket and started leafing through the contracts.

"Oh, never mind now. You can mail my copy." She didn't want a reminder of what she'd agreed to do; on the drive home she only wanted to enjoy being with him for a little while longer.

Greg was in high good humor, regaling her with a steady stream of lighthearted comments, but for Martha the joy had gone out of their trip. She didn't want to be his employee; signing the contract was only a way to stay in his life. Her mother's mind would be put at ease and for that she was grateful, but she was consumed with longing to hear three simple little words from him: I love you.

Greg checked plane reservations as soon as they got back to Alexandria. She wanted to go with him to the airport but it wasn't the practical thing to do. He had to drive the rented car to leave it there; she'd either have to follow in her car or take a cab home. They decided to say good-bye at her house.

The evening was dry and pleasant. The courtyard was filled with the fragrance of spring; the fresh scent of budding bushes and damp earth lingered even after the sun went down. They sat on the splintery old bench, holding hands and exchanging light little kisses until the time came when he had to leave.

"I'll call you soon," he promised.

"When will that be?"

"Tomorrow night, probably. We have a lot to talk about."

He nuzzled her ear like a magician doing a familiar trick; the outcome was the same, but it didn't make her happy. She didn't want him to leave her!

"I could go with you," she suggested in a low, scared voice.

"And sit around in my apartment while I work twenty hours a day catching up? That's more distraction than I can handle this time, darling. Anyway, the sooner you finish your cookbook, the more time you'll have to help launch Martha's Inns. Keep thinking of entrees for the menu, won't you?"

"All right."

"Ah." He groaned loudly.

"What's wrong?"

"I have so much to do, I hardly know where to begin."

"Start by catching your plane," she said.

Mistaking the tension in her voice for levity, he laughed. "I can depend on you to be practical."

That wasn't a compliment to hold in her heart during the long, empty days that followed.

Martha wasn't an actress; she tried to sound cool and nonchalant when she told her mother about signing Greg's contract, but her face was a dead giveaway.

"You really don't want this job, do you?" her mother asked.

"I'd be crazy not to take it. There's no way in the world I could earn that much money any other way."

"You won't have time to do any more cooking programs here."

"A few guest appearances on local TV don't mean that much to me."

Her mother frowned as though trying to remember something. "The Sugar Glen cookbook. When will you find time to finish it?"

"It's nearly done." This was a slight exaggeration.

"You only signed because of my medical bill," her mother said unhappily.

"No, there were other reasons." At least this was the truth, although Martha didn't intend to explain about wanting to stay in Greg's life.

"I wish you'd talked to me before signing the contract," Fleury said, sounding very much like a mother now. "I'd feel so much better if Carl had read it."

Impatient now because she recognized the wisdom in what her mother was saying, Martha tried to drop the subject. "It's too late to change my mind now."

Greg called the next evening just as she'd lost hope of hearing from him and decided to go to bed.

"I'll be in Michigan for a couple of days, then Indiana and Ohio," he said.

"Why?" She didn't expect his answer to make her happy.

"We're negotiating to buy out a small chain of restaurants. It'll mean we can launch Martha's Inns that much sooner."

"In the Midwest?" She'd been imagining the colonial dining rooms in places like Alexandria or Williamsburg.

"Sure, here the colonial theme will be a novelty. In the East it's old hat."

"You don't want your food compared to authentic colonial cookery?" She wasn't enjoying this conversation; Greg had yet to say one personal thing.

"I hadn't thought of it that way." He didn't hide his irritation; she wasn't proud of herself for asking.

"When will I see you again?"

"I don't know. I may not have time to call you for a few days, but I'll be in touch."

Their call ended abruptly; he was angry because she'd questioned his motives for beginning in the Midwest. Their business relationship was looking less and less promising; their personal relationship wasn't going anywhere either.

Burying herself in work filled the days but did nothing for her peace of mind. Being apart from Greg was torture, but their brief telephone conversations every few days were anything but loving exchanges. He sometimes said "miss you" or bemoaned the fact that his work kept him away from her, but he never suggested that she join him.

Meanwhile, the first draft of her book, which the Sugar Glen board had enthusiastically approved, went to the printers. So far, much to her relief, no one had complained about the recipes she'd omitted. Fortunately she'd found a usable one from every member who'd contributed to the project.

Before the book was finished, she'd be responsible for checking and rechecking the contents and proofreading with an exacting eye for accuracy, but as far as her daily routine was concerned, she was done. Ordinarily she would've been actively soliciting further assignments, contacting historical societies, presenting programs, and writing articles. But with Greg's work looming ahead, she wasn't motivated to return to any of her usual activities.

Their separation time lengthened; it would soon be three weeks of absence from Greg, twenty-one long, empty days without feeling his arms around her or his mouth kissing hers. He still called every few days but instead of conversation, he gave her progress reports.

Filling her time, as well as fulfilling one of Greg's requirements, she studied hundreds of recipes, trying to decide whether they had the potential to feed large numbers of people in a commercial operation. She checked out every book she could find in the library on quantity cooking and restaurant management but one thing was missing from all her activity: excitement. Laboring over economical recipe conversions couldn't compare to the thrill of discovering one long-forgotten recipe.

Her copy of the contract finally came in the mail; she turned it over to her mother to study but didn't reread it herself. She'd find out all too soon what was involved in being the Martha of Martha's Inns.

"We're opening a new Mr. Turkey near Richmond," Greg said in a late-night call. "I thought I'd fly in for it and we can go together."

"Do you make a personal appearance every time a new franchise opens?"

"No, but it's good public relations. You know, the franchises stay under our wing, so to speak. We contract for all their supplies, handle the advertising—"

"Yes, I understand how a franchise works," she said, wanting to hear that he missed her, not that he was coming to help secure his already vast fast-food empire.

"My plane arrives at three something. I'll rent a car and come to your house."

"I can meet you, and we can use my car."

"Never mind, it's just as easy to get a rental. My secretary made all the arrangements."

Of course, he didn't want to rely on a car as old as hers. She wondered whether his secretary was young or old, beautiful or dowdy. Undoubtedly she was efficient. A typed itinerary for the Richmond visit arrived by express mail the next day. The only thing it didn't document, she thought, was whether she was supposed to share a room with Greg for the one night they'd be gone.

Seeing him on her own front step was like being transported back to the country inn in New Jersey. She was in his arms, and days of longing were wiped out.

"Oh, baby, did I miss you!" he said between hungry kisses, hugging her so vigorously he took her breath away.

"You never told me!" Now that she was in his arms, there was no bite in her accusation.

"How can I talk to a cold phone receiver when what I need is a warm woman in my arms?"

"A warm woman!"

"Not any woman, silly. Only you!" He kissed her soundly. "You, you, you."

"I missed you too." Her voice told him how much.

"Is your mother home?"

"No, she went to her therapy session. She's able to drive by herself now."

"When will she be home?"

"Late tonight. She's going to a friend's for dinner."

Martha didn't know how her mother, the matchmaker, had managed that invitation, but for once she loved her for it.

"I missed you so much," he repeated, letting his tongue wander in the curlicues of her ear, driving her wild with warm, moist thrusts.

Without talking about it, he took her hand, running up

147

the stairs to the second-floor landing, then up to her cozy room on the third floor.

Neither of them stopped to think. His beautifully tailored gray suit fell in a heap on her waxed floorboards with the rest of his clothing, and it never occurred to her to worry whether her blue linen-weave suit would be too wrinkled for travel.

They tumbled onto her quilt-covered bed, exchanging urgent, consuming kisses, touching, holding, delighting in each other, until, with ragged breathing and trembling bodies, they came together.

Old springs cried out as the frantic motion pinched them together. Even the venerable floor joists squealed in protest, but Martha and Greg were caught up in the fury of a hurricane, lost in a rapture too long denied.

Lying shoulder to shoulder with arms and legs touching, they floated together in a state of perfect euphoria, forgetting that the world existed outside of her snug nest.

He fondled her intimately, letting his fingers wander over peaks and valleys, rekindling her desire while her mind was still numbly satiated.

"You're so nice," she murmured. Really, being in love was an incredible delight. She thought of telling this to Greg but her mouth was otherwise occupied.

"Now do you believe I missed you?" he teased.

She demanded more proof.

Later, lying under her quilt, knowing that they soon had to leave for Richmond, they held hands and talked.

"It's hard to realize how old this house is," he mused. "Did your ancestors really live here?"

"One branch did. The house passed out of our hands for a while, but my great-grandfather bought it back."

"My great-grandfather got off an immigrant boat with a name I can't even pronounce now."

"Kent isn't your real name?"

"Now you know my darkest secret," he said, laughing softly. "No one in the immigration service could pronounce Gramp's name, so he changed it on the spot."

She was a little shocked that anyone would throw away their family name but didn't want to ask questions since Greg usually seemed uncomfortable talking about his background. Greg closed the subject by getting up.

"We've got a restaurant to open."

"Not until tomorrow."

"No, but your mother will be home pretty soon."

"I don't think she'd care if you're here."

"No, but she'd *know,*" he teased, mimicking the words she'd said many weeks earlier.

She didn't know what he'd told his secretary but there was definitely only one room reserved for them in Richmond.

The gala ceremony was scheduled for eleven A.M., just before the noon hour rush, but Greg wanted to be there early.

"You'll get to meet Mr. Turkey," he said, admiring her as she finished dressing in her red suit.

"Don't tell me! Who is he really?"

"An actor named Brad Silkirk, although sometimes we use substitutes. In the costume it doesn't matter."

The parking lot was full an hour before the ceremony was scheduled, but Martha soon found out why. Mr. Turkey was there with a whole crew of helpers passing out free balloons to the kids, doing his tail-heavy stomp, dancing on oversized rubber feet to music provided by a three-piece band.

"Yuck, yuck, yuck," Mr. Turkey cried out, cavorting in front of the entrance still barred to the public by a wide yellow ribbon. "Yuck, yuck, yuck."

149

Martha was pretty sure he was imitating some famous laugh but she couldn't identify it.

"He seems to enjoy himself," she said dryly.

"The kids like him." Greg led her around to a service entrance, then spent some time introducing himself and her to the new employees waiting to go into action. Turkey burgers and fries were stacked to capacity under warmers in anticipation of a run on the opening day special. Through the large glass windows in front she could see Mr. Turkey hopping up and down on one foot and waving his arms like a bird with a broken wing.

"We don't have to stay too long," Greg assured her. "I have to say a few words outside introducing the owner, then he has some local beauty contest winner—Miss Peach Blossom or something—lined up to cut the ribbon."

"Fine," she said, forcing herself to sound enthusiastic.

The ceremony began on time. A traffic jam around the new glistening-white restaurant with blue roof tiles made it imperative that they get things moving.

Greg was wonderful with people, making his speech sound like a friendly welcome to friends. Mr. Turkey led a round of applause, flapping a tail that belonged on an alligator. Then Miss Peach Blossom cut the satin ribbon and handed the scissors back to Greg, conveniently tilting her head so he could plant a big kiss on her ruby-red lips. Martha pretended to be engrossed in Mr. Turkey's latest number, something that involved a fowl version of a nursery rhyme.

What would happen when Greg started opening Martha's Inns? This question alone was enough to ruin her day; she pretended not to see the woman she'd dubbed Miss Balloon Bosom hanging on every word Greg said.

It wouldn't be Mr. Turkey opening the first Martha's

Inn; the job would be hers! Just imagining the possibilities gave her a bad case of stage fright. She'd be wearing some costume designer's version of a colonial dress, but instead of hiding behind a turkey disguise, she'd have to stand there and be herself, telling a crowd how the restaurant was serving food just like Martha Washington's. Telling whoppers like that to a crowd of strangers in Sandusky, Ohio, or Warren, Michigan, would be bad enough, but going on national television, letting members of every historical society in the country see her promoting a fast-food restaurant would be disastrous. She could get a doctoral degree in history and no one would take her research seriously anymore.

Greg finally detached himself from the beauty queen and took Martha's arm.

"I'm through now. Have you seen enough?"

She'd seen enough to send her hitchhiking back to Alexandria!

"I'm ready to go," she said, keeping her thoughts to herself.

Before getting into the rental car, Greg took off his suit jacket and laid it on the back seat.

"I have to go to Cincinnati and see some people tonight. There won't be time for me to change," he said.

"You're flying out of Washington today?"

"With no time to spare," he said regretfully.

She had an overnight case borrowed from her mother; there was no reason why she couldn't go with him.

"You could come with me," he suggested.

"You won't be too busy for me?"

"Things are falling into place. No, that's a lie. I'm going to have to work my tail off in the next couple of weeks. I just don't want to be without you that long."

Sitting behind the steering wheel, he reached over and

took her hand, separating the fingers, kissing her knuckles and caressing the skin between her fingers with the tip of his tongue.

"You're going to miss your plane."

She didn't want to melt in his arms; it wasn't fair of him to attack her senses with his considerable battery of seductive tricks, not when he hadn't staked a claim on her love.

"Come with me," he said more urgently.

"Last time you didn't want me."

"Like hell I didn't! I just thought there wouldn't be time for us to be together. I didn't realize how hard it is not being with you."

Remembering Miss Balloon Bosom gave her courage. "Surely you have other friends."

"Girlfriends?" He laughed. "Do you want to know what my love life has been like since I met you?"

She did, desperately, but couldn't bring herself to admit it.

"You're special, Martha," he said gently. "There's not another woman in the world I want to be with right now."

"Right now" spoiled it all.

"And later?" she asked, afraid of his answer.

"This isn't a good time for me to think ahead," he said quietly. "You don't know how much is involved, getting an enterprise like this off the ground."

He started the car, cautiously making his way through the traffic only beginning to thin around the new Turkey Haven.

When they were free of urban tie-ups, headed back toward Alexandria on I-95, he asked her again. "Come with me."

152

"No. The pages will be coming back from the printers. I have a lot of proofreading to do."

"Just stay with me a couple of days."

"I really should take care of my cookbook."

She was going to regret her decision a thousand times in the long days and nights to come, but hanging on the fringe of his life, waiting for him to clear a few hours to be with him, wasn't a way she could live.

"You're going to have to go to work for me yourself pretty soon," he warned after several minutes of silence. "I'm having Stan Hayes, my publicity man, orchestrate your role."

"Do you mean I'll be working with him?"

She'd always imagined working side by side with Greg, being his righthand woman. It was her main reason for signing the contract.

"Yes, he'll be contacting you."

"I thought you . . . I mean, you and I—"

"I don't run a one-man show," he said dryly.

"Well, you have time to buy eggs in Ooookola!"

"Oskaloosa. I only went there because I needed some time away to think."

"What kind of contract does Mr. Turkey have?"

"Basically the same as yours."

She insisted on riding to the airport with him. If he took her home, there was a possibility he'd miss his plane. His good-bye kiss wasn't as warm as those he'd given her on his arrival.

"Do you have cab fare home?" he asked just before boarding time.

"Yes, of course!"

"You're sure—"

"Greg, I can get home on my own."

"I'll miss you."

His last kiss was a little more emphatic but she was hurting too much to enjoy it.

Was love supposed to make a woman happy?

She took the subway home because she didn't have enough for a cab. The efficient new urban line brought her within blocks of her home, but she was embarrassed to be walking home with her mother's overnight bag. She felt like a fancy lady sneaking home after being tossed over by some cad.

"Greg," she said to herself, "I wish I didn't love you."

Her fingers were crossed.

CHAPTER NINE

"I'm not as happy as I should be," Rhonda said.

They were leaving a house sale where, only minutes before, Rhonda had been thrilled to buy an eighteenth century candle snuffer. Martha was used to her friend's exaggerated complaints and noisy but short-lived bouts of misery over trivial things, but this quiet, understated sentence worried her.

"What's wrong?"

"Nothing, nothing at all. That's the trouble."

They walked along a tree-shaded village street to Rhonda's car, and she loaded the purchases destined for her aunt's antique shop into the trunk.

"Are you and John having—" Martha began when they were seated.

"No, nothing like that! He's a love! I wouldn't trade him for the world."

"Then I don't understand."

"Neither do I. We have a lot of fun together. I wouldn't leave him for anything."

"Then what?" Martha felt protective toward her friend; it was totally unlike Rhonda to sound unsure of herself.

"I'm floating. That's it. I'm floating along on the surface of things. No goals, no plans, no aspirations. I'm tired of my own parties."

That, Martha could understand!

"Maybe after your vacation trip this summer—"

"A couple of weeks in British Columbia won't change anything." Rhonda turned the key in the ignition, impatiently grinding the starter.

"I know how you feel."

"You couldn't possibly!" Rhonda always liked to believe her problems were unique. "You're about to start a thrilling new career. If there's anyone I know who isn't stuck in a rut, it's you!"

"I'm not sure promoting restaurants is right for me."

This was the first time she'd confided in Rhonda about her misgivings. Her friend was so interested, she forgot her own problem.

"You can't be serious?"

"Dead serious. Can you see me singing 'Yankee Doodle' and hopping around like Mr. Turkey at a restaurant opening?"

"You won't be doing anything that silly."

"I'm not so sure."

"You always were a little shy," Rhonda said with an annoying authority born of many year's friendship. "Remember when we were juniors? You were the only one in our group who wasn't in the talent show."

"I couldn't dance on a sprained ankle!"

"That's what you said, but anyone can wrap an elastic bandage around an ankle."

"I don't believe you! All these years you thought I faked a sprained ankle?"

"Well, exaggerated it. Remember how you got sick to your stomach the first time you had to give a speech in speech class?"

"I had a touch of flu!"

Rhonda was making her feel guilty! Had she used little

upsets and emergencies as a way of avoiding unpleasant duties?

"Maybe."

"Well, what I did or didn't do in high school has nothing to do with working for Greg."

"I'd do a tap dance in a mermaid costume for an opportunity like yours. Imagine, having a whole chain of restaurants named after you!"

"They're named after Martha Washington!"

"I'm sure! A man who used to go through women like tissues suddenly starts hanging around Alexandria and naming restaurants after you."

"You don't know what you're talking about," Martha grumbled.

The cookbook was history, at least until that distant day when she could enjoy the royalties. Warm weather arrived, and Martha tackled the garden, pulling dead vegetation and working until her palms had blisters from clipping branches. With the back door open, she could hear the phone ring, but the expected summons to begin work for Greg didn't come.

He called late that night. "Things are looking good," he said. "Stan Hayes will be calling you any day now."

"When will I see you?" It was her number one concern, plaguing her days and haunting her nights.

"It can't be too soon for me," he said, but he didn't set a date.

"I'm working in the garden." This was her subtle way of telling him she didn't have a darn thing to do.

"Did you get a check?"

"Yes, but I'd like to be doing something for it."

"The contract calls for monthly advances. You'll be

earning them soon." He rattled off a list of cities where the first Martha's Inns would open.

"Are you going to open them the way you do Turkey Havens?"

"My publicity people are working on that. Naturally we want as much attention as possible."

"Naturally."

Her head felt stuffy; she must be getting a cold. Remembering what Rhonda had said about imagining little ailments to get out of things in high school, she sniffled loudly and decided it was only an allergic reaction from pulling weeds.

"I'll be in Detroit for a few days," he said.

"Will you call?"

"I'll try but we'll be spending long hours in conference."

"Call any time."

"You can't hear the phone on the third floor. I'd only wake your mother."

"Well, I miss you." She didn't care if she sounded pouty.

"I miss you," he said automatically.

The first menu arrived by express mail a few days later; it was the standardized one that would be used by all the Martha's Inns as they opened. Beginning to read it, she felt much as she did whenever the first copy of one of her cookbooks arrived. Here was the culmination of her efforts.

The good feeling faded quickly as she scanned the menu. A few of her recipes had been incorporated into the dinner selections: fried clams, chicken pie, smoked Virginia ham. But most of the entrees were the ordinary ones found in thousands of restaurants: pork chops, steak sandwiches, fried chicken. Diners couldn't order her favorites: spoonbread, sweet potato soufflé, or currant cake. It wasn't much compensation to find apple tarts on the dessert list.

She called Greg that evening, trying again and again until she got him in his hotel room in Detroit.

"I received the menu," she said.

"What do you think of the cover?" he asked excitedly.

"The cover was very nice," she said stiffly, "but I thought you were using more of my recipes."

"We used several—apple tarts, clams—"

"Not my oyster stew."

"Sweetheart, not many people want real cream these days. Too many calories, too much butterfat."

"Too expensive?"

"Certainly that too."

"You could've told me you'd only use a few of my suggestions. I thought I'd be endorsing a menu I helped put together. I sent you hundreds of choices."

"I had a crack research team go over each and every one."

"Still, I thought—"

"Martha, there's nothing in your contract about planning the whole menu."

"Yes, but you could've told me!"

"You didn't even read the contract before you signed it! I told you to have your lawyer go over it."

"Oh, I'm sure you're right legally. But—"

"But you're disappointed, and I'm sorry. There's just no way I can create a popular chain of restaurants without costing out every item, studying the marketing reports my staff prepares, relying on professional judgment—"

"All right," she said dejectedly. "I guess I'm lucky you like my apple tarts."

"Your apple tarts aren't the only thing I like," he said softly. "Pretty soon I'll be out of the woods on this. We can spend some time together."

Only some time? she wanted to say. Instead she broke off the call, sleeplessly nursing her disappointment far into the night.

Greg used charm to accomplish his ends; Stan Hayes, his publicity director, used brashness. His harsh eastern accent grated on Martha's nerves after a minute of conversation on the phone; she hated to think of working with him for days, weeks, maybe even months.

"The first thing is to get some advertising stills," he said. "We'll get started at ten A.M. tomorrow. Write this address down."

She did, then realized what he was suggesting. "That's in New York City, isn't it?"

"Sure. Look, bring along a few copies of your books. We may work them in somewhere."

"Just a minute! It's after four o'clock. Do you expect me to be in New York tomorrow morning?"

"You got it."

"I may not be able to get a flight."

"My secretary has a ticket for you. I'll turn you over to her when we're through."

Martha was almost through before she started, but at seven A.M. she was on a plane, not at all cheered by Fleury's instructions to have fun.

The photographer's studio was on the top floor of a converted warehouse.

Stan was waiting for her there with a photographer he introduced as Iggy.

"I rented two costumes," Greg's man said. "Let's try them both and see which fits the Martha's Inn image. I

160

think I'm gonna like the red better, but the green has something going for it."

The green laced in front, but it didn't help to tug the strings tightly together. The neckline ended just above her navel. Only a girlie magazine would run an ad with that dress, she decided, hurriedly taking it off.

The red wasn't much better; there must have been eighteen yards of cloth in the skirt, draped over a framework of wires, but the designer only used about eight inches for the bodice. Her breasts swelled over the tops exactly like ripe melons.

"Neither will do," she said, coming out from behind the screen that served as a dressing room.

"Have to," Stan said. "No time to get another."

Iggy leered.

"This isn't the way a colonial cook looked. A dress like this was only for fancy balls—in Paris!" She fussed with the wrist ruffle that nearly covered her hand.

"That has nothing to do with it," Stan said.

Greg hadn't used her cherished eggplant recipe, she recalled, staring at the irate publicity man.

"I think I'd better talk to Greg," she said.

"Be my guest."

He gestured to a table phone and Martha started dialing. Greg's secretary accepted her collect call but couldn't tell her how to reach him.

"He left Detroit this morning but isn't expected here until late afternoon. May I have him call you?"

"No, thank you." She turned to Stan. "He's not in his office. We'll just have to postpone."

"You can't postpone Iggy. He's getting two hundred an hour for the sitting and the meter's running."

She managed not to gasp. "This dress is cut too low."

161

"We can fix that later. Paste in a little ruffle or something on the proofs."

"I'd rather have a little something now." She looked more carefully at the lace on her wrists; it was loosely sewn with large basting stitches. "Do you have some scissors?"

She tried not to notice that it took her over fifty dollars worth of Iggy's time to remove the lace cuffs and tuck them in where they'd do more good. The filmy trim was see-through, but bunched together between her breasts, it helped some.

"It looks silly," Stan complained.

The wig he made her wear looked sillier. A heavy structure of artificial white hair, it made her look like one of Louis the Fifteenth's mistresses.

"Martha Washington never wore anything remotely resembling this," she said.

"Martha Washington never launched a new line of restaurants," Stan said.

Iggy got on with the business of taking five thousand shots under lights that made her steam, then droop, in the airless loft. Her neck muscles ached from supporting the heavy wig in the most unlikely postures, and the lacy ruffle tucked between her breasts stuck damply to her skin. She held a platter of artificial mauve-colored ham until looking at it made her feel queasy, and smiled her welcoming smile until her face muscles ached all the way to her ears.

Considering the amount of the check she'd deposited a few days ago, she couldn't complain of being exploited, but she heartily believed that this job was completely wrong for her.

She stayed overnight at the Plaza; she had to look for-

162

ward to making a television commercial the next day. Greg called that evening.

"Everything going okay?" he asked cheerfully.

"Greg, I'm not very good at this!"

"Sure you are, sweetheart. Stan said the stills are dynamite."

"You're making that up!"

"Well, he grumbled a little about some lace ruffle. Said the costume you tore may cost us two thousand dollars, if you ruined it."

"Oh, no! I carefully removed the lace from the wrists because it was needed somewhere else. I didn't hurt the dress at all. I felt naked the way it was."

Instead of forgiveness, she got a dry little laugh.

"I have big news," he said.

The only thing she wanted to know was when they'd be together again.

"The first opening has been scheduled. Battle Creek, Michigan, on the Fourth of July."

"Battle Creek?"

"Yes."

"So soon?"

"I can't wait to get this off the ground. You should be through there in a few days. Can you meet me in Cincinnati, say on Thursday? I'll have my secretary arrange a flight for you."

"Greg . . ." She was bursting to tell him how she felt about what was happening, but neither of them was very good at speaking their minds over the phone. It would be much better to talk to him in person.

"No problem, is there?"

"Not about meeting you, I guess."

"You don't sound enthusiastic."

"Oh, I really want to see you," she assured him.

163

"Me, too, darling, me too."

Stan arranged for a different costume to make the commercial. *Authentic* wasn't in his vocabulary, but his persistence was wearing her down. All she really wanted was to be done with posing, with saying "Welcome to Martha's Inn," with smiling under a quarter inch of makeup and a twenty-pound wig. She hoped the ham wouldn't look purple on national TV. She could imagine the members of the Sugar Glen Historical Society watching her promote ham that looked like grape gelatin.

Her mother met her at International Airport and didn't say a word when Martha burst into tears watching other people's luggage spill off the conveyor belt.

"I did something you may not like," Fleury said when Martha's tears had dried and they were on the way home.

"Are you sure you want to tell me?"

"I'd better. Carl came over for dinner the other night."

"He does that quite a bit, doesn't he?"

"You do like him?"

"Of course! If you like him, I'm crazy about him."

"Well, that's beside the point. We had lovely lamb chops. I braised them just the way you showed me."

"Mother!"

When Fleury began with a long, involved preface, Martha braced herself for the worst.

"Well, we are becoming good friends, Carl and I. There didn't seem anything wrong in having him glance at your contract."

"There's no point in it!"

"Well, as it turns out, there wasn't."

"What did he say?"

"You won't like it very much."

"I'm sure I won't," Martha said dejectedly.

"He said Kent Enterprises has you sewn up seven

164

which ways. The contract is a masterpiece—from an attorney's point of view."

"Great."

"He did say you're going to make a lot of money."

She couldn't believe how little she cared.

Airports brought out the worst in people; they talked louder, walked faster, and ignored each other more pointedly than in any other public place. Martha hated flying alone; she worried about departure gates, boarding passes, and delayed arrivals as though her life depended on them.

Maybe her life did depend on seeing Greg again; certainly her happiness did. She had to explain to him that she wasn't at all good as a TV personality or as a model. He probably realized it already. He'd be the first to see the horrible results of her trip to New York.

He was waiting for her in Cincinnati, in a fawn colored suit, looking as appealing as she remembered him. His hair fell in soft waves over his ears and forehead and she thought there were several new threads of silver. As always, his skin had a healthy glow heightened by the whiteness of his stiff collar and he moved toward her with quick, sure steps, the walk of a man totally in command of his world.

"Hello." He smiled down on her, his face animated with pleasure. "It's been too long."

"Yes, it has."

People kiss all the time in airports; it's a nice way to say good-bye or welcome someone home. Usually no one pays any attention, but their kiss was a traffic-stopper. Martha didn't even realize it.

"Guess what?" he said after they'd claimed her bag and were walking to the exit.

"I'm not good at guessing."

165

"You are very good in front of a camera. The tape of your commercial came this morning."

"You've seen it?"

"At least ten times! It's great!"

It wasn't what she wanted to hear.

"I have a rented recorder in my motel room. I can't wait to show it to you."

"Greg, there's no hurry." The sound she made was a weak attempt at a laugh.

"I have your stills, too, but we may have to do them over. I haven't decided yet."

"Do I owe you for the costume?"

"I don't know. It doesn't matter."

"It matters to me. I don't go around destroying people's property. If they charged you for repairs, I want to pay."

"I can't keep track of every little detail. The important thing is, you look great on TV. You can see for yourself. I have a car over here."

In the parking lot the sun reflected off the chrome and glass of hundreds of autos, making her squint as she practically ran in high heels to keep pace with Greg. He was too excited about showing her the tape to notice.

While Greg fiddled with the rented VCR in their motel room, she turned off the air conditioner, then turned it back on low when she discovered the windows wouldn't open.

Watching herself on videotape was one of the last things she wanted to do now that they were together.

"You never sound so Southern in person," Greg teased, sitting on the foot of the bed beside her, totally absorbed in her brief performance on tape.

"Thank you," she said dryly, remembering all the con-

166

fusing directions that had bombarded her during the taping.

On the screen she was picking up the platter of purple ham; it didn't look any more appetizing on television.

"The ham should be pinker," she said.

"I don't think anyone will notice."

She knew what viewers would notice. Once she'd thought being amply endowed was an asset; now it seemed embarrassing. The pseudo-colonial dress had done just what she'd feared: pushed her breasts practically up to her chin and made them look unnaturally large.

"I hate that dress!" she said vehemently.

Greg looked at her in surprise. "It looks fine."

"You mean it looks sexy! I'm supposed to be a food expert endorsing your restaurants, not a—a—"

"You can be an expert and still look attractive," he said mildly.

"There's nothing attractive about that wig! It makes my face look like a doll's."

He laughed.

"It's not funny, Greg. That person isn't me!" She pointed at another take of the commercial flitting across the screen. "And I can't stand the things I'm saying! Real Virginia ham is slowly cured in a smoke house—"

"I wasn't planning to serve slices of the plastic prop!"

"Don't joke. I'm serious."

"I can see that, but you're making a big fuss over nothing. The tape is great."

"Great! All anyone will see is that ridiculous wig and my . . . and the front of my dress."

"I'm pleased with this tape." His tone of voice was unyielding.

"You can't use it!" She glared at the screen, blank now that the tape was done. "It's just too tacky."

"I can't use it?" He raised one eyebrow and his face held nothing but challenge. "You really should've read your contract more carefully."

"I know you *can* use it, but I don't want you to." Losing her temper wasn't going to help, but holding back was a strain.

"Let's look at the stills. Those probably should be redone."

Martha didn't think the black and white glossy photos were nearly as bad as the tape.

"Was it your idea to bunch all that cloth in the front of the dress?" Greg asked, sounding none too pleasant.

"I couldn't have my picture taken in a dress that—"

"If you had something to be ashamed of," Greg interrupted, "I might be about to understand some of this fuss. But cameras make you look beautiful. I suspected they were kind to you when I saw that little local show you did."

"You mean the camera flatters me?" She was angry, not fishing for compliments.

"I didn't mean it that way! You know I think you're beautiful. I meant that most people aren't as photogenic as you are."

He stepped close and touched her cheek with the back of his hand. "I don't want to fight about this," he said softly.

"I just want the commercials to be . . . ." She groped for the right word. "Dignified."

His laugh annoyed her more than anything he'd said.

"There's nothing funny about that!"

"Dignity doesn't sell dinners! The people who come to my restaurants aren't wealthy gourmets. They're just ordinary hardworking people who want a little fun when they can afford a meal out."

"So you want me to look like a tavern wench, not a colonial lady?"

"If you want to put it that way, yes." He walked to the machine and removed the tape. "I have what I want right here. The stills won't do with rags stuffed in front of the dress. Next time do it the way Stan says."

She couldn't have been more stunned if he'd hit her. The corporation head who issued orders and expected them to be obeyed was a stranger to her.

"Let's go out for dinner," he said in his normal voice. "I haven't had a bite all day."

Too dazed to know what she wanted to do, she numbly followed him.

He suggested going to a first-class seafood restaurant; she insisted on eating at a fast-food place called Happy Marvin's.

"Is this some kind of punishment for liking your tape?" he asked, picking some rather doughy batter from his order of fish.

"I don't know what you mean," she replied, still chewing a bite of her tough steak sandwich.

"Making me eat here to prove you're one of the common people too." He seemed amused, which only made her more angry.

"There's nothing like a nice folksy restaurant." She shifted uncomfortably on the garish orange plastic seat of the booth.

"Are you going to pout all evening because I think you're wonderful?"

"I'm not pouting." She bit into another chunk of gristle and tried discreetly to remove it from her mouth behind a paper napkin.

"Tell you what. Let's go back to the motel and order their club sandwich. I had one last night. Thin slices of nice moist turkey, crispy bacon, tomatoes, and lettuce that's been washed—"

"Stop that!"

"Well, that's what I'm going to do." He wrinkled his nose and pushed away his barely-touched platter of fish and thick greasy fries. "If you want to get a doggy bag so you can keep chewing on that warmed-over shoe leather—"

"You think you're terribly clever, don't you?" She'd never known him to be so sarcastic, and she hated it.

"Let's go. I'm too tired for this."

He did order a club sandwich from room service, but she refused to eat any of the inviting little triangles made with cracked wheat bread. Instead she took an overly-long shower, trying to decide just how mad she was.

When she finally emerged from the bathroom, steamed pink and with her hair curling damply, it really didn't matter whether she was still angry. Greg was sound asleep on top of the bedspread, in his unbuttoned dress shirt and white briefs, so deeply asleep that he didn't stir when she covered him with a light blanket and turned out the lights. She crawled unhappily under the sheet on the other bed.

When she awoke, the shower was running. Her watch showed that it wasn't quite seven, but Greg was never one to sleep late. She wanted him beside her, smooth-cheeked after his shave, his skin sweetly scented by soap and his specially-blended cologne, the hair on his body still damply matted from bathing. Soon he'd walk into the room flicking a towel over his torso, using two hands to run it down the length of his spine, over round, sexy buttocks. Then he'd come to her.

Imagination alone was enough to make heat flow through her; clutched by a familiar longing, she longed for the moment when the door opened and Greg came to her. Instead of lying there, she summoned all the strength in her character, forcing herself to sit on the edge of the bed, then stand and move to her suitcase.

She'd slept the way Greg liked: just as she'd been born. Hastily pawing through her suitcase, she found clean panties and bra, dressing with all possible haste. By the time the bathroom door opened, she was fully dressed in tailored white slacks with a casual navy cotton jacket. After stepping into her white pumps with spiky little heels, she turned to say good morning.

"You're dressed. I thought . . ."

She knew what he thought. He tied a white bath towel around his waist, but not before revealing what was on his mind.

"I thought we should talk," she said stiffly, averting her eyes.

"Sorry I fell asleep last night. I haven't been getting much sack time." He sat on the edge of one bed and reached for her hand, but she moved away.

"It doesn't matter."

Maybe it was a good thing, she thought. She felt the same way Rhonda did: not as happy as she should be. Nothing was going quite the way she'd hoped.

"Of course it matters!" He stood and walked over to her, circling her with his arms, massaging the end of her spine in the way that drove her wild.

"Please don't, Greg."

"If that's what you want." He stepped back and watched her with narrowed eyes, his face totally unreadable.

"What I want . . ." She couldn't finish her thought aloud. "I didn't know things would be this way."

"What way is that?" He sat on the edge of the bed and crossed his arms over his bare chest.

Just the sight of his shoulders, firm and honey-hued, was enough to wipe her mind clear of troubling thoughts, but she had to speak now. They spent too little time together to waste this opportunity.

"I see you so seldom." That was her real sorrow. "And now, doing the commercials . . ."

"What about them?"

"I didn't understand how it would be."

"If you have questions, ask them. I'm not a mind reader."

Being deprived of his morning pleasure seemed to have made him testy.

"You didn't tell me how it would be." He didn't tell her that she'd only be an occasional diversion, someone he turned to when he had a few free hours.

"Representing Martha's Inns?"

"Yes." This was the part she could talk about.

"Everything is spelled out in your contract. I urged you to have your own attorney go over it."

"My contract doesn't say I have to make commercials wearing a tavern wench's costume. You never told me anything about that!"

"Be reasonable, Martha. The gowns are a little low-cut, but they're no worse than wearing rubber feet and turkey wings. People won't buy food from a stuffy lecturer. All I do is merchandise my businesses in the usual way."

"I thought Martha's Inns would be different."

"Are you saying you find working for me distasteful?"

"Yes! I hate being your pin-up girl!"

172

"You're being ridiculous. You have a lucrative contract. Just because you can't dictate the way the ad campaign is going, you're acting like a spoiled child."

"Is that what you think?" She jerked away from his grasp and retreated to the far side of the room.

"I think," he said wearily, "that this argument is pointless. I don't even know what you want."

"I just want to do my job with some semblance of dignity!"

"There's that damn word again! Dignity! You make it sound like I've asked you to do something terrible, something degrading and humiliating! All you have to do is wear a period costume and say a few lines. I've put my reputation on the line to launch these restaurants and all you have to do is say a few nice things about them."

"That's just like you! Gloss over the problems! There are so many things you've never told me!"

"I'm trying to find out what!"

She was crying too hard to tell him. Never, never, never had she had a fight like this with another human being. How could people survive, fighting with the one they loved? That was the most important thing Greg had neglected to tell her: whether he loved her.

She ran to the bathroom and locked the door, patted a cold cloth on her face until her cheeks were numb, and finally came out, only because she'd decided what to do.

Greg was dressed in a three-piece beige suit; looking hurt and troubled only added to his moody attraction.

"I'm going home," she said in a flat, dull voice that masked the seething turmoil behind it.

"I wish you wouldn't. We can work this out."

"How?"

"I didn't say I have all the answers!" he snapped.

173

Martha knew she didn't have any.

"I'm leaving now," she said bleakly. "You don't need to drive me to the airport."

He watched, not saying a word as she left.

CHAPTER TEN

Instead of seeing the little nosegays of pink flowers on the wallpaper in her room, she saw the yellowing background and the frayed spots along the seam lines. The narrow cracks between the shrunken floorboards seemed like gaping slits, and the ceiling was oppressively low. It didn't matter that now she could afford to strip the room to a bare shell and recreate it any way she liked. The thought of spending Greg's money only plunged her more deeply into a sea of regrets.

Greg didn't know the real Martha, she thought. She hadn't let him see enough of her true self to understand her reluctance to work for him. He didn't have the slightest notion that she was sacrificing something to become a promoter, a huckster. The fault was hers; she'd been pretending to be someone else. The red suit, the nights of love, and her signature on the contract were all part of her deception. The woman Greg wanted wasn't the real Martha Graves.

She knew she had to live up to the terms of the contract; she didn't have to give in to her love for Greg. Even without Carl's opinion of the contract, she wouldn't try to break it. No one had forced her to sign it; she'd recklessly ignored Greg's warning to have her own attorney evaluate it. More importantly, her word was good. Because she'd agreed to the job, she would do it. She could handle that.

What she couldn't handle was an on-again, off-again love affair with Greg. The woman who met him in motels and settled for a few scattered nights of love wasn't being true to herself or fair to him. Nothing good could come to either of them if they continued. Sooner or later her unhappiness would drive him away.

She was absolutely sure this painful decision was the right one. All that remained was to let Greg know. The solution seemed to be a letter. At least she'd have the satisfaction of breaking off their relationship before he did the same thing by totally ignoring her. She hadn't heard from him since she'd left Cincinnati almost a week ago. But there was no real comfort in rejecting Greg, not when all she really wanted was to be his forever.

She tried again and again that evening to write the perfect letter, but nothing said quite what she intended. There was no way to swear allegiance to a restaurant chain and break off an affair in the same letter without revealing some of her own pain and frustration. When she heard her mother coming up to bed, she gave up, deciding to tackle the problem the next day.

The phone rang in the middle of the morning, while Martha was halfheartedly dusting the living room, one of a series of jobs she'd undertaken to avoid getting back to the letter. Would the day ever come when she could hear a ring without hoping it was Greg? Again this morning her hopes were dashed; the call was for her mother.

"I can't believe it!" Fleury came into the living room, still limping but moving with surprising alacrity. "I just can't believe it!"

"What?"

Her mother seemed to be a hundred percent happier

176

these days but Martha couldn't imagine what caused this outburst.

"You won't believe it!" Her mother impulsively hugged her.

"Carl proposed?"

"Oh, no." Her mother's cheeks changed color with something suspiciously like a blush. "We're not going to rush things. At our ages we don't want to make a mistake. But this is Carl's doing."

"What is?"

"The doctor in Baltimore isn't going to sue us for the rest of his fee. Carl convinced him to drop it because the publicity would hurt his reputation."

"You mean we don't have to pay his bill?"

"Absolutely not! Carl says this sometimes happens after the Peer Review Committee decides a doctor has overcharged. I guess no one likes to be criticized by fellow professionals. Isn't that wonderful news!"

"Wonderful!" Martha smiled, happy for her mother but not sure how she felt about Greg's contract now. Would she have signed if the Baltimore doctor had relented a few months earlier? She didn't want to think about it!

"There's one other thing I should tell you," her mother said, sounding almost shy.

Martha went on dusting the legs on the TV stand.

"It looks like I'll be able to go back to work part-time in a few weeks."

Martha was fresh out of "wonderfuls." She was happy for her mother but too emotionally drained to react.

"Once I start, I'll probably be pretty tired for a while, so Carl thought—that is, Carl invited me—just for a little break."

Her mother came as close to stuttering as she'd ever heard her.

"Is something wrong?"

"Oh, no! Carl just wants me to fly to Quebec for a few days. With him," she added meekly.

"Are you asking my permission?" Martha's smile gave her away.

"Of course not! Oh, you're still a terrible brat sometimes! I just want you to be happy for me. I mean, playing bridge and visiting friends is fun but—"

"There should be a little more to life than that?"

"There hasn't been anyone for a long time," her mother said in a subdued hush.

"Go for it, Mom!" Martha kissed her cheek, soft and powdery under her lips, and wondered which of them was cutting the apron strings.

When she was young, she imagined that their house had a ghost, a friendly spirit who only wanted to be part of the family. Maybe this had been her childish version of an imaginary friend. The next day she wished she could believe in her little spectral companion again. Her mother had departed early in the morning and the house seemed bleakly empty.

The only bright spot in the day had been when Rhonda had called with joyous news—she was going to have a baby! Martha hadn't heard her friend sound so happy in a long time and was delighted for her. Now Rhonda would have not only a husband and stepchildren to love, but her very own baby.

Rummaging through the refrigerator, Martha found a plastic bag of large ripe peaches. Believing that cooking or baking was the best way to forget her troubles, she decided to make her favorite tarts. Maybe tomorrow, she thought, she'd have a couple of friends over to share them. What sense did it make to mope around as though she didn't have a friend in the world?

She sighed. What good did it do to kid herself that any number of people could fill the void created by Greg's absence?

As the tarts baked, they left a marvelous spicy, fruity smell in the kitchen. It really was uncomfortably warm by the time they were done, so she escaped to the courtyard with a book. In the summer their old iron lawn furniture was scattered around outside. They hadn't been freshly repainted this year but the faded orange and yellow flowered seat pads her mother had sewn long ago were still comfortable. There were worse ways to spend a summer evening than reading in this tranquil spot.

The first bang on the iron gate startled her into dropping the book; the successive knocks frightened her. Who was pounding so furiously on the old gate?

She had to walk around the corner of the house to see down the narrow length of the passageway that led to the sidewalk and street.

"Are you going to let me in?"

Greg was standing behind the bars of the gate, grasping one in both of his hands, glaring down the shadowed passageway. "I rang at the front door," he said as she slowly made her way between the closely-situated brick walls of the Graves house and the neighboring one.

"I didn't hear. I was sitting out back."

"Are you going to open the gate?" he asked more softly.

"Yes, of course." She'd tried to communicate with him in dozens of unfinished letters. Now that he was here, she couldn't remember a thing she'd decided to say.

"Thank you," he said, when her fumbling efforts finally released the lock.

She led the way to the courtyard.

"I was in the neighborhood so I thought I'd drop in," he joked weakly. "Your garden is nice."

The courtyard was the nicest thing about the house in the summer, when azaleas, magnolias, and crape myrtle blossomed, each in its turn. He sat on the edge of the splintery gray seat circling the ancient boxwood. She perched on a little padded iron footstool, pulling her knees up and resting her chin on them.

There'd been no greeting between them; he'd followed her down the passageway without touching her, although she felt his eyes on her back and felt self-conscious in her skimpy white shorts.

"How've you been?" he asked like a polite stranger.

"Fine."

"Your mother?"

"She hopes to go back to work soon, at least part-time."

"I'll go in and say hello." He stood, stretching like a traveler who's been confined in one position for a long while.

"She's not here."

"Oh?"

"A friend asked her to go to Quebec for a few days." It didn't sound right to say her mother had gone away with a man.

"It smells nice here."

"Yes, it does."

He paced across the flagstones, as though measuring each with the length of his stride.

"How did you get here?" she asked.

"Plane from Chicago. Rented a car at the airport." His bored tone told her there was nothing more to discuss on this subject.

180

"I didn't know when I'd see you."

"You know what they say about bad pennies."

She didn't. "I wrote you a letter—tried to."

"Did you mail it?"

"No."

"Should I read it now?"

"No, I tore it up—I tore all of them up. Can you believe it, a writer who can't finish a letter?"

He nodded his head sympathetically. "Like a business man who botches his biggest deal."

"You aren't having difficulty with your new restaurants?"

"No, they'll probably be the most successful thing I've done."

"I'm glad." She didn't want him to fail.

"I have something for you in the car. Do you mind if I go get it?"

"No."

"You'll let me back in if the gate shuts?"

"I'll come hold it for you."

The rented blue Chevy was right in front of her house; she seemed to be the only one who never found a free spot there. Greg opened the trunk and took out a paper-covered bundle about the size of a ten-pound bag of flour. Up close his package appeared to be covered with a layer of brown grocer's paper, then white sheets and a layer of plastic.

"I carried this onto the plane with me," he emphasized. "It was one thing I didn't want to end up in the land of lost luggage."

He walked ahead of her into the courtyard, then stopped by the kitchen door.

"Am I invited in?"

"Of course," she said, beginning to remember all the things she intended to tell him.

"I couldn't be sure." He shrugged his shoulders. "After Cincinnati."

"Come in," she said coolly, only beginning to realize how hard it would be to tell Greg that their personal relationship was over.

"Have you had dinner?" he asked, laying his bundle on the tiled work counter.

"No." Not even freshly baked tarts had tempted her; her loss of appetite had something to do with feeling as if her heart were in her throat.

"What smells so good?" He looked toward the table where the tarts were cooling on a rack beside her two uncut loaves of rye bread. "Apple tarts?"

"Peach."

"Perfect." He started busily unwrapping his package, which proved to be a large ham. "Virginia ham. I may have to corner the market on them."

"You're going to serve the real thing?"

"At every Martha's Inn. You get the first slice."

"I made rye bread."

"Then all we need is some mustard."

He found the sharpest carving knife in a rack over the stove, carefully testing the edge on his thumb before tackling the succulent ham. His technique was faultless; in much less time than Martha would've taken, he had thin, perfect slices arranged on a platter.

"We'll serve it a little thicker at Martha's Inn," he said, "but I like my sandwich meat thin."

"Did you come all this way to bring me a ham?" she asked, beginning to experience a peculiar light-headedness that she attributed to forgetting to eat all day.

"I told you, I just happened to be in the neighborhood."

The ham had been prepared by a master; every bite was tangy with a texture that was faultless.

"It's saltier than I like my food," Greg said, biting into his second sandwich.

"Um, I can tell you're really having to force yourself." She refilled his glass with milk, another thing she'd never seen him consume.

"I won't have to force myself to try your tarts. You aren't saving them for anything special, are you?"

"I thought I might have some friends over tomorrow evening."

"How many friends?"

She hadn't asked anyone yet. "Just a few, three or four."

"Four friends plus you is five. You baked twelve tarts, so allowing one apiece—how many of your friends are men?"

"Why do you ask?"

"Men are more apt to take seconds, so allowing one each for the women and two for the men, how many tarts can I eat?"

"You sound like a greedy little boy. Eat as many as your conscience allows."

"My conscience has been tormenting me lately; I prefer to ignore it. Are you having any men eat my tarts?"

"Your tarts!"

"I'm talking first-come, first-serve." He arranged three on a clean dessert plate she'd provided.

"I haven't invited anyone yet," she admitted, amazed at Greg's appetite. She thought of him as a fastidious, almost picky eater who rarely overindulged.

He broke off a bite of golden-sweet tart, the top swimming in her special sour cream mixture. "This is even better than your apple tarts."

"Apples are best when they're freshly picked in the fall. I'm surprised you're eating so much."

"Another dark secret. Inside this body there's a fat man struggling to get out."

"Will he make it?"

"I hope not. I only stuff myself when I need courage."

"Courage?" She looked up from the tart she'd been crumbling with her fork. "Why would you—"

"Because I used up my considerable store of nerve just coming here." He abandoned his fork and studied her with a vulnerable, open expression. "I haven't been so scared since I got this." He fingered the fine white scar on his chin.

"Greg, about the letter I tried to write—"

"Let me wrap the rest of the ham, then we can talk in the living room."

"I can do it."

"No, let me."

"You know what you're doing in the kitchen."

"My father had the kind of grocery store where he sliced the lunch meat to order for the customer. He had the best Polish sausage on the South Side. Made it himself."

His beige suit jacket was hanging on the back of a kitchen chair and he worked at clearing away the meal in a short-sleeved white dress shirt. The remains of their meal soon disappeared; he didn't look at her while he worked.

This was the man she was going to send away forever! Her hands were so shaky she had to keep them hidden on her lap and a loud voice was drumming inside her: fool,

184

fool, fool! If one of her letters had been in her hand now, she would've eaten it.

"Come into the living room," he invited.

She went, scarcely remembering that this was her home. When she was seated on one end of the couch, she tried her voice just to see if the power of speech still belonged to her.

"Did you have a good flight?"

"A good flight!" he exploded. "I'm so sick of chasing all over the country—"

"I'm sorry I asked!"

"No, I'm sorry." He sat beside her, sideways so he could look at her, taking one of her hands in both of his. "I'm mad at myself because I'm such a tongue-tied idiot sometimes."

Greg was as articulate as anyone she knew; she stared at him in puzzlement, wondering again why he'd come.

"I've thought a lot about your contract," she said slowly. "I realize you're not asking me to do anything that wasn't included in it. You won't have any more trouble with me."

His groan was hardly what she'd expected.

"You win!" she said. "I'll do whatever you like."

"Tear the damn thing up!"

"What?"

"My copies were wrapped around the ham. They're in your trash can now."

"You don't mean that?"

He dropped her hands. "Don't look that way. I'll still honor it, if that's what you want."

"I don't understand." She couldn't have been more confused if he'd been speaking Chinese.

"My number-one rule has always been to keep my

185

business and personal life separate. In college I wouldn't even date the waitresses who worked in my pizza place."

"It was a mistake for us to—"

"No! Darling, I won't hold you to the contract."

He sounded so miserable, she instinctively reached out and clutched his hand.

"For years," he said softly, "everything I had went into my business. The odds were all against me when I started. My turkey idea was laughed out of more banks than I can count. Building Turkey Havens took all my time and thought. There wasn't room for anything else in my life. Do you understand what I'm trying to tell you?"

"Your work was all that mattered?"

"Yes, and then it started to be less important. I was only playing around with the idea of a new chain when I met you. You made the whole thing fall together."

"I really am the Martha in Martha's Inns?"

"From the beginning!" He squeezed her hand. "Boy, am I botching this! I'd fire anyone who wasted this much time getting to the point."

He fell silent for a moment, then stood, looking down on her. "The point is, I love you too much to hold you to the contract if it isn't what you want."

Tears welled up in her eyes, then she was in his arms. His kiss was sweet and deep, claiming her as his, while tears trickled down her cheeks and moistened his.

"Have I made you unhappy?" He touched the dampness on her face, taking out his handkerchief to blot it.

"No, I cry when I'm happy."

"Silly habit," he teased, gently kissing away the rest of her tears, brushing her lids with his lips.

"I don't want to let you down. I'll do anything you want to promote the Inns," she said.

"You're not a very good listener!"

186

How could she be, when his fingers were caressing the back of her neck, sending shockwaves of pleasure down the length of her spine.

"I signed it so I could be with you," she admitted both to herself and to him, hurriedly confessing before her nerve totally failed her.

"I was afraid of that. But you don't need a contract to be with me, darling. I love you too much to be apart from you."

Her shoulders were trembling and she was afraid to believe that, at long last, he was saying the things she'd been dying to hear.

"I love you too," she said, hiding her face against the front of his fine cotton shirt.

"You don't have any brothers or sisters?" he asked suddenly.

"No, but what—"

"Who else will restore the family manse if we don't?"

Her heart was beating with excitement. "This house?"

"We won't live here all the time—only when the weather's better here than in Chicago."

"The weather's always better here than in Chicago! What do you mean *we?*"

"Central air conditioning is the first thing this house needs." He unbuttoned his shirt and slipped out of it.

"Talk straight, Gregory! You never tell me enough!"

"You never listen! I love you!"

"And you want to live here?"

"No, only visit without collapsing from the heat. You'll want to see your mother once in a while, won't you?"

He sprang suddenly, tumbling her on her back on the couch and pinning her down with his legs.

"No!" She pushed him away, but not too far away. "I'm listening!"

"I'm offering you a contract you won't need to have checked by a lawyer. I'll see that you never want to break it."

"I've had one contract from you."

"All right, I'll spell it out!" He sat up. "Marry me, darling."

She sat up next to him and saw an expression of troubled earnestness on his face. "Yes," she whispered in a voice filled with emotion.

"I've been scared to death you'd say no. You do mean it?"

"Yes, I do."

"I've never proposed before—not marriage, not to anyone."

"You were too busy."

"Too obsessed with building my own little empire."

"Hold me."

She didn't need to ask twice.

With her cheek pressed securely against Greg's shoulder, she couldn't resist asking, "Did you really like the tape I made?"

"Only enough to watch it a couple of hundred times."

"If it means that much to you, I'll still live up to my contract."

"You'd do that for me?"

"Yes." And so much more, she thought.

"I want you with me, as my wife. The business doesn't need you as badly as I do."

"I want to be a help to you."

"Scratch my ribs. Right there. Um, wonderful."

"I mean a real help."

"You are, darling, you are. I junked the menu. You made your point at Happy Marvin's. Martha's Inns will

188

need all the help you can give to serve authentic colonial cooking."

"Greg, that's wonderful! And if you want me to represent them—"

"No, I want you to be Mrs. Kent. I'll even tell you my great-grandfather's real name." He whispered it in her ear, making her giggle.

"That funny?" he asked.

"No, you tickled my ear, and you know what that does to me."

"No more of that until we write the bottom line."

"What bottom line?"

"We hire a professional model to do the promoting."

"To do the commercials?"

"Yes, and to open the restaurants."

"I won't have to sing 'Yankee Doodle'?"

"Only in the shower."

"I get to choose her costumes! That's my bottom line!" She ran her fingers through his tousled hair, thinking again how beautiful it would be as it turned to a dazzling silver. "You're going to be a handsome old man."

"Distinguished?"

"Definitely."

"Greg."

"Um."

"Tell me again."

"I'll never stop telling you. Darling, I love you." He buried his face in her hair. "I love you."

"Rhonda's going to have a baby."

"Oh?" He nuzzled her throat. "That's nice."

"Do you really think so?"

"Sure." He sat up and looked into her face. "But I'll be a lot more excited when you're the one with a bun in the oven."

"You want to be a father?"

"Of course! Children run in my family. My mother may stop thinking I'm useless when I'm a father."

"She doesn't think that?"

"No, I think she adores me—in secret."

"I cut some apron strings today."

"How?"

"I sent my mother off for the weekend with a man."

They laughed until they felt weak, forgetting what was funny, only knowing that being together was very, very sweet.